Mayne Reid

The Lost Mountain

A Tale of Sonora

Mayne Reid

The Lost Mountain
A Tale of Sonora

ISBN/EAN: 9783743338715

Manufactured in Europe, USA, Canada, Australia, Japa

Cover: Foto ©Andreas Hilbeck / pixelio.de

Manufactured and distributed by brebook publishing software
(www.brebook.com)

Mayne Reid

The Lost Mountain

THE COYOTERO CAMP.—p. 58

THE

LOST MOUNTAIN

A TALE OF SONORA

BY

CAPTAIN MAYNE REID

LONDON
GEORGE ROUTLEDGE AND SONS
BROADWAY, LUDGATE HILL
NEW YORK: 9 LAFAYETTE PLACE
1885.

CAPTAIN MAYNE REID'S BOOKS.

"There was not, we believe, a word in his books which a schoolboy could not read aloud to his mother and sisters."—*Standard*.

CONTENTS.

―⁓∧∧∧⁓―

THE LOST MOUNTAIN.

CHAPTER I.

IN WANT OF WATER.

"*MIRA! El Cerro Perdido!*" (See! The Lost Mountain!)

The man who thus exclaims is seated in a high-peak saddle, on the back of a small sinewy horse. Not alone, as may be deduced from his words; instead, in company with other men on horseback, quite a score of them. There are several wagons, too; large cumbrous vehicles, each with a team of eight mules attached. Other mules, pack animals, form an *atajo* or train, which extends in a long

1

line rearward, and back beyond this a drove of cattle in charge of two or three drovers—these mounted, as a matter of course.

The place is in the middle of a vast plain, one of the *llanos* of Sonora, near the northern frontier of this sparsely inhabited state. And the men themselves, or most of them, are miners, as might be told by certain peculiarities of costume, further evinced by a paraphernalia of mining tools and machinery seen under the canvas tilts of the wagons. There are women seen there too, with children of both sexes and every age; for it is a complete mining establishment on the move from a *veta*, worn out and abandoned, to one late discovered and still unworked.

Save two of the party all are Mexicans though not of like race. Among them may be noted every shade of complexion, from the ruddy white of the Biscayan Spaniard to the copper-brown of the aboriginal, many being pure-blooded Opata Indians, one of the tribes called *mansos* (tamed). Distinctive points of dress also, both as to quality and cut, denote difference in rank and calling. There are miners *pur sang*—these in the majority; teamsters who drive the wagons; *arrieros* and *mozos* of the mule train; *vaqueros* with the cattle; and several others, male and female, whose garb and manner proclaim them household servants.

The man who has called out differs from all the rest in costume as in calling, for he is a *gambusino*, or professional gold-seeker. A successful one, too; since he it is who discovered the *veta* above spoken of, in the Great Sonora Desert, near the border-line of Arizona. " Denounced" it as well—that is, made declaration and registration of the discovery, which, by Méxican law, makes the mine his own, with exclusive right of working it. But he is not its owner now. Without sufficient means to undertake the *exploitation*, he has transferred his interest to those who can—Villanueva and Tresillian, a wealthy mining firm, long established near the town of Arispé, with all their *employés* and a complete apparatus for excavating, crushing, and amalgamating—furniture and household gods added—are *en route* for the new-found lode, with high hopes it may prove a "bonanza." It is their caravan that is halted on the plain, for to halt it has come at a hail from the *gambusino* himself, acting as its guide.

He is some distance in advance of the wagons with two other horsemen, to whom his speech is particularly addressed. For they are the chiefs of the caravan—the masters and partners of the mining company composing it. One of them, somewhat over middle age, is Don Estevan Villanueva, a born Mexican, but with features of pure Spanish type, from his Andalusian ancestry. He is somewhat the senior of the two, and senior partner of the firm, the junior being Robert Tresillian, an Englishman, and native of Cornwall.

Up to that moment there had been anxiety on the countenances of both, as on those of their followers, indeed more, a look of gravest apprehension. Its cause is apparent; a glance along the line of animals—ridden horses as well as draught and pack-mules—clearly proclaiming it. All show signs of distress, by sides hollowed in, necks outstretched and drooping, eyes deep down in their sockets, and tongues protruding from lips that look hot and dry. No wonder! For three days they have not tasted water; and the scant herbage of the plains, on which they have been depasturing, is without a particle of moisture. It has been a season of drought all over Sonora, not a drop of rain having fallen for months, and every stream, spring, and pool along their route dried up. Little strange, then, the animals looking distressed, and no more that the minds of the men are filled with gloomy fears as to what might be before them. Another three days, and it may be death to most, if not all.

Just in like proportion are their spirits uplifted on hearing the exclamation of the *gambusino.* Well know they what it means—good grass and abundance of water. All along has he been telling them of this, picturing the

"Lost Mountain," or, rather, a spot by its base, as a very Paradise of a camping-place. No want of water there, he has said, however dry the season or long-continued the drought; no fear of animals being famished, since not only is there a spring and running stream, but a lake, surrounded by a belt of meadow-like land, with grass thick, succulent, and green as emeralds.

"You're sure it's the Cerro Perdido?"

It is Don Estevan who thus doubtingly interrogates, his eyes fixed on a solitary eminence seen afar over the plain.

"*Sí*, señor," affirms the guide, "sure as that my name's Pedro Vicente. And I ought to be sure of that, from what my mother told me; the old lady in her life never getting over her anger at the cost of my christening. Twenty silver *pesos*, with a pair of church candles—big ones, and of best wax! All that for only handing down to me my father's name, he being Pedro, and a poor *gambusino* as myself! *Carramba!* The *padres* are the veriest extortioners—levy black-mail more rigorously than either footpad or highwayman."

"*Vaya, hombre!*" rejoins Don Estevan. "Don't be so hard upon the poor priests. And as for the expense your mother was put to in celebrating your baptismal rites, that's all past and gone. If you were poor once, you're now rich enough to care nothing for such a trifle as twenty dollars and a couple of wax candles."

The senior partner speaks truth, as any one who had seen Pedro Vicente three months before, seeing him now, would say. Then was he sparely clad, in garments of faded hue, tattered and dust-stained; his mount the scraggiest of mustangs—a very Rosinante. Now bestrides he a horse of best blood and shapely proportions, in a deep tree-saddle of stamped leather, with ornamental housings; his own body bedight with all the glittering adornments peculiar to that special Mexican dress known as "*ranchero,*" picturesque as any in the world. His lucky find of gold, still in its matrix of quartz—*madre de oro*, as the Mexican miners call it—with its transference to Villanueva y Tresillian, has given him sufficient of this same metal with the mint stamp on it for all matters of comfort, costume, and equipment.

"Oh! bother your christening and candles," puts in the Englishman, with a show of impatience; "we've something more serious to think about. You're quite sure, Señor Vicente, that yonder eminence is the Cerro Perdido?"

"I've said," laconically and somewhat gruffly answers the guide, showing slightly nettled at the doubt cast on his affirmation, and by one he supposes a stranger to the country and its ways --in short, a "*gringo.*"

"Then, pursues Tresillian, "the sooner we get to it the better. It's ten miles off, I take it."

"Twice ten, *caballero*, and a trifle over."

"What! Twenty miles? I can't believe that."

"If your worship had been roaming about these *llanos* as long as I have, you could and would," rejoins the guide, in quiet confidence.

"Oh! if you say so, it must be. You seem

to know, Señor Vicente; and should, from all
I 've heard of your skill as a path-finder. That
you 're good at finding gold we have the
proofs."

"*Mil gracias*, Don Roberto," returns the *gambusino*, with a bow, his *amour propre* appeased
by the complimentary speech; "I 've no doubt
about the distance, for I 'm not trusting to guess-
work. I 've been over this ground before, and
remember that big *palmilla*." He points to a
tree at some distance, with stout stem, and a
bunch of bayonet-like leaves on its summit—a
species of *yucca*, of which there are several
straggled over the plain, but this one taller than
any. Then adds, "If your worship doubts my
word, ride up to it, and you 'll see a P and V
carved in the bark, the initials of your humble
servant. It was done to commemorate the
occasion of my first setting eyes on the Cerro
Perdido."

" But I don't doubt your word," says Tresillian, smiling at the odd memento in such an
out-of-the-way place ; "certainly not."

"Then, señor, let me assure you that from it to the mountain is all of twenty miles, and we'll do well if we get there before sundown."

" In which case, the sooner we start for it the better."

"Yes, Pedro," adds Don Estevan, speaking to the gold-seeker in a friendly, familiar way. "Ride back and give the order for resuming route. Tell the teamsters and all to do their best."

"At your worship's command," returns the *gambusino*, with a bow, and wave of his broadbrimmed hat raised high over his head.

Then, pricking his horse with a spur having rowels full five inches in diameter, he canters off towards the caravan.

Before reaching it he again uncovers, respectfully saluting a group which has not yet been introduced to the reader, though possibly the oddest, with the individuals comprising it, the most interesting of all the travelling party. For two of them are of the fair sex—ladies—

one middle-aged and of matronly aspect, the
other a girl late entered upon her teens. Only
their faces and the upper portion of their forms
are visible, for they are inside a sort of palanquin
—the *litera* of Mexico, used by grand dames on
long journeys, and roads over which carriages
cannot be taken. The face of the older lady,
with dark complexion and features of Andalusian type, is still attractive, but that of the
younger one strikingly beautiful ; and between
the two is a strong family resemblance, as there
should, since they are mother and child—the
Señora Villanueva and her daughter.

The *litera* is borne betwen two mules, attached to shafts fore and aft, in charge of a
strapping fellow in velveteen jacket, and *cal-
zoneras*, *botas* of stamped leather, and *sombrero*
of black glaze, with a band of silver bullion
round it. But there is a fourth personage comprising the group, unlike all the others, and
bearing no resemblance to any of the way-
farers save one—the Englishman. To him the
youth—for young he is—shows the likeness,

unmistakable, of son to father; and such is the
relationship between them.

Henry Tresillian, just turned seventeen, is a
handsome fellow, fair-haired, of bright complexion, and features delicately chiselled, still
aught but effeminate in their expression; instead, of a cast which proclaims courage and
resolution, while a figure tersely knit tells of
strength and activity equal to anything. On
horseback, he sits bending over in his saddle
with face to the curtains of the *litera*. There
may be eyes inside admiring him; and the expression of his own tells he would fain have it
so. But all their eyes, late full of gloom, sparkle
delightedly now. The Lost Mountain has been
sighted; their fears are over, and so soon will
be their sufferings.

"*Anda! adelante!* (advance)" shouts Pedro
Vicente.

His words echoed rearward along the line,
followed by other cries, with a creaking of
wheels and a cracking of whips, as the wagons
once more got into motion.

CHAPTER II.

THE "COYOTEROS."

THE moving miners are not the only travellers making for the Cerro Perdido on this
same day. Just as they have sighted it, approaching from the south, another party is
advancing towards it from the north, though
not yet within view of it, from being farther
off, with a swell of the plain interposed.

Very different in appearance, and, indeed,
almost in every respect, is this second band
from that already introduced to the reader; in
count of men outnumbering the latter by more
than treble, though in bulk as a moving mass
far inferior to it. For with it are no wagons,
nor wheeled vehicles of any kind; no mule train
nor cattle drove. Neither are they encumbered
with women and children, least of all a *litera*

13

and ladies. All men, and every one of them on horseback, each bearer of his own baggage, as well he may be, so little and light it is. Their sole *impedimenta* consist of a few trifling commodities, chiefly provision wallets, with water gourds (*xuages*) strapped over their shoulders or tied to the wither-locks of their horses. Equally unobstructive is their garb, few of them having other articles of dress than a breech-clout, leggings, and moccasins, with a rolled-up blanket or *serape* in reserve. The exceptions are some half-dozen, who appear to exercise authority, one especially holding command over all.

His insignia are peculiar ; a coat of arms that would puzzle all the heraldic colleges of Christendom. Nor does he wear it on his shield, though one he carries. It is borne on his naked breast of bronze black, in a tattooing of vivid red ; the device, a rattlesnake coiled and couchant, with tail and head erect, jaws wide agape, and forked tongue protruding ready to strike. Beneath are other symbols equally eloquent of

anger and menace; one in white, set centrally,
well known all over the world—the "death's
head and crossbones."

It need hardly be said that he, embellished
with this savage investiture, is an Indian, and
his following the same. Indians they are, of a
tribe noted for bloodthirstiness beyond all others
of their race; for they are the Wolf-Apaches,
or Coyoteros, so called because of mental and
moral attributes which liken them to the
coyoté—jackal of the Western world.

Unaccompanied by their women and children, as unencumbered with baggage, proclaims
them on a warlike expedition—a *maraud;* their
arms and equipments telling of the same. They
carry guns, and long-shafted lances with pen-
nons attached, that no doubt once waved above
the heads of Mexican *lanzeros.* Pistols too,
some even having revolvers, with rifles of latest
pattern and patent; of which by their way of
handling them they well know the use. If
civilization has taught them nothing else, it has
how to *kill.*

They are marching along, not in ruck, or straggling crowd, but regular formation, aligned in rank and file, "by twos." Long since have the Horse Indians of both prairie and pampa learnt the military tactics of their pale-faced foes —those special to cavalry—and practise them. But nowhere with more ability and success than in the nothern states of Mexico—Tamaulipas, Chihuahua, and Sonora — where Comanches, Navajoes, and Apaches have charged in battle line, breaking that of their white adversaries, and scattering them as chaff. · "Indian file," oft used as a synonym for "single file," is a march formation long since abandoned by these Transatlantic Centaurs, save where the nature of the ground makes it a necessity.

None such exists on the open *llano*, where this Apache band is now ; and they might move in a column or extended line, if willing it ; but numbering scant two hundred, they prefer the double file. Unlike the miners, in their three days' traverse of a waterless desert, they have been making way through a district with which they are familiar; acquainted with all the camping-places—every stream, spring, and pond—so they have not suffered from want of water. Nor are they likely now, since their course lies along the banks of a creek—a tiny rivulet, yet running, despite the continued drought. It is a branch of the Rio San Miguel of the maps—locally known as the Horcasitas—and they are descending it southward, thirst having no terrors for them.

Just as the sun is about to set they catch sight of the Cerro Perdido. To them it is not known by that name, but *Nauchampa-tepetl.* Somewhat strange this, pointing to an affinity known to exist between the Indians of Northern Mexico and the Aztecans of the South. In the language of these last the mountain Peroté bears the same designation, the "Cofré" usually attached being synonymous with "Nauchampa," both signifying chest, or box. For the Cerro Perdido, viewed from certain points, bears a quaint resemblance to this, as does also the summit of Peroté.

Neither philology nor ethnography is in the minds of this band of red-skins; their thoughts are dwelling on a subject altogether different —robbery and murder. For they *are* on the maraud; their objective point the towns on the Horcasitas.

Just now, however, as they sight the Cerro, another question occupies them : whether it be prudent or possible to continue on to it without halting for the night. Some say Yes, but most No. It is still good twenty miles off, though appearing scarce ten. In the diaphanous atmosphere of the Sonora tableland distances are deceptive, as Pedro Vicente has said. But the native inhabitants, above all the aborigines, are aware of this, and reckon accordingly. Besides, the Coyoteros, like the *gambusino*, have been over the ground before, and are familiar with every foot of it. So distance has nought to do with their discussion, save as it affects the capability of their horses. Since morning they have made fifty miles, and are fagged ; twenty more would be killing work for them. And the twenty to Nauchampa-tepetl will be a nice distance to their next day's noon halt.

The question of continuing on is at length decided in the negative, by him of the grotesque heraldry dropping down from his horse, and proceeding to picket the animal on the grass. As his example has the force of a command, all the others follow it, and camp is quickly formed. A simple affair this; only the tethering out of their steeds, and stripping them of such caparison as they carry. Then follows a search for dry faggots, and the kindling of a fire; not for warmth, but cooking. There is a bit of butchering to precede; these red-skinned rovers having their commissariat on the hoof—this in the shape of some spare horses driven along *en caballada*. A knife drawn across the throat of one lets his blood out in a torrent, and he drops down dead,—to be skinned and cut up in a trice, the pieces impaled upon sticks and held over the blaze of the fire.

But the hippophagists avail themselves of other comestibles of a vegetable kind; seeds from the cones of the *piñon*, or edible pine, and beans of the *algarobia*—trees of both sorts growing near. Enough of both are collected and roasted, to form an accompaniment to the horseflesh.

Fruit they find too on several species of cactus; the best of them on the *pitahaya*, whose tall rigid stems, with limbs like the branches of a candelabrum, tower up around their camp. So, in the desert—for it is such —they are enabled to end their dinner with dessert. To provide something for breakfast besides, a viand rare and strange, but familiar to them, a branch of their tribe—the " Mez-caleros "—making it their staple food, even to deriving their tribal appellation from it. For it is the mezcal plant, one of the wild species of magueys (*Agave Mexicana*). The central core, from which radiate the stiff spinous blades, is the part eaten, and the mode of preparing it is now made manifest in the Coyotero camp.

Several plants are torn out by the roots, their leaves hacked off, and the skin of the core itself cut away—leaving an egg-shaped mass of white vegetable substance, large as a man's head, or a monster mangold-wurzel. Meanwhile, a hole has been "crowed" in the ground, pit-shaped, its sides fended by flat stones, with a like pavement at the bottom. Into this red coals are flung, nigh enough to fill it; an interval allowed for these to smoulder into ashes, and the stones become burning hot. The mezcals, already wrapped up in the horse's skin late stripped off, red side inward, along with some loose pieces of the flesh, and the bundle is lowered down into the improvised oven, then all covered over with a coat of turf. Thus buried it is left to bake all night, and in the morning will afford them a meal Lucullus need not have disdained to partake of.

The Coyoteros, well sure of this, go to sleep contentedly and without care; each rolled up in his own wrap, his couch the naked earth, canopied by a star-bespangled sky.

In that uninhabited and pathless wilderness,
or with paths only known to themselves, they
have little fear of encountering an enemy; and
as little dream they that within less than two
hours' gallop of their camping-ground is another
camp occupied by the foes of their race, too
few to resist their attack. Knew they but this,
there would be a quick uprising among them,
a hasty springing to horse, and hurried ride
towards Nauchampa-tepetl.

CHAPTER III.

MEANWHILE, with many a crack of whip and cry of "*Anda!*" "*Mula maldita!*" the miners have been toiling on towards the Lost Mountain. At slow pace, a crawl; for their animals, jaded and distressed by the long-endured thirst, have barely strength enough left to drag the wagons after them. Even the pack-mules totter under their loaded *alparejas*.

Viewing the eminence from the place where they had pulled up, the mine labourers, like the Englishman, had been inclined to doubt the guide's allegation as to the distance. Men whose lives are for the most part spent underground, are as sailors ashore when above it, oddly ignorant of things on the surface, save what may be learnt inside a liquor saloon.

23

Hence their unbelief in Vicente's statement was altogether natural. But the mule and cattle-drivers knew better, and that the *gambusino* was not deceiving them.

All come to this conclusion ere long, a single hour sufficing to convince them of their mistake; at the end of which, though moving continuously on, and making the best speed in their power, the mountain seems far off as ever. And when a second hour has elapsed, the diminution of distance is barely perceptible.

The sun is low down—almost touching the horizon—as they get near enough to the Cerro to note its peculiar features; for peculiar these are. Of oblong form it is; and, viewed sideways, bears resemblance to a gigantic catafalque or coffin, its top level as the lid. Not smooth, however, the horizontal line being broken by trees and bushes that stand in shaggy silhouette against the blue background of sky. At all points it presents a *façade* grim and precipitous, here and there enamelled by spots and streaks of verdure, wherever ledge or crevice gives plants of the scandent kind an opportunity to strike root. It is about a mile in length, trending nearly north and south, having a breadth of about half this; and in height some five hundred feet. Not much for a mountain, but enough to make it a conspicuous object, visible at a great distance off over that smooth expanse of plain. All the more from its standing solitary and alone; no other eminence within view of it, neither *sierra* nor spur; so looking as if strayed and *lost*—hence the quaint appellation it bears.

   *   *   *   *   *

"At which end is the lake, Señor Vicente?" asks the elder Tresillian, as they are wending their way towards it; he, with Don Estevan and the guide, as before, being in advance of the wagon train.

"The southern and nearer one, your worship. And luckily for us it is so. If it were at the other end, we'd still have a traverse of a league at least before reaching it."

"How's that? I've heard that the Cerro is only a mile in length."

" True, señor, that's all. But there are rocks strewn over the *llano* below, for hundreds of yards out, and so thick we couldn't take the wagons through them.   I suppose they must have fallen from the cliffs, but how they got scattered so far, that puzzles me, though rocks have been the study of my life."

" So they have, Pedro," put in Don Estevan. " And you 've studied them to some purpose. But let us not enter into a geological discussion now.   I feel more concerned about something else."

" About what, your worship ? "

" Some memory tells me that Indians are accustomed to visit the Cerro Perdido. Though I can see no sign of human being about it, who knows but there might be ? "

This is said after examination of the plain all along the base of the mountain through a field-glass, which Don Estevan habitually carries on his person.

" Therefore," he continues, " I think it advisable that some five or six ride ahead—those who are best mounted—and make sure that the coast is clear. In case of red-skins being there in any formidable numbers, the knowledge of it in time will enable us to form *corral,* and so better defend ourselves should we be attacked.

Before becoming a master miner, Don Estevan had been a soldier, and seen service on the Indian frontier, in more than one campaign against the three great hostile tribes, Comanches, Apache, and Navajo. For which reason the *gambusino,* instead of making light of his counsel, altogether approves of it — of course volunteering to be himself of the reconnoitring party.

In fine, there is another short halt, while the scouts are being selected; half a dozen men of spirit and mettle, whose horses are still strong enough to show speed, should there be Indians and pursuit.

Of the half-dozen, Henry Tresillian is one; he coming up quick to the call. No fear of his horse giving out, or failing to carry him safe back if pursued, and whoever the pursuers. A noble animal of Arab strain it is, coal-black, with a dash of dun-colour between the hips and on either side of the muzzle. Nor shows it signs of distress, as the others, notwithstanding all it has come through. For has not its young master shared with it every ration of water served out along the way, even the last one that morning?

In a few minutes the scouting party is told off, and, after receiving full instructions, starts onward.

The elder Tresillian has made no objection to his son being of it; instead, being rather proud of the spirit the latter is displaying, and follows him with admiring eyes as he rides off.

Still another pair of eyes go after him, giving glances in which pride and fear are strangely commingled. For they are those of Gertudes Villanueva. She is proud that he, whom her young heart is just learning to love, should possess such courage, while apprehensive of what may come of it.

"*Adelante!*" calls out the *mayor-domo*, who

has chief charge of the caravan; and once more there is a vigorous wielding of whips, with an objurgation of mules, as the animals move reluctantly and laboriously on.

*   *   *   *   *

In twenty minutes after, all is changed with them. Horse and hybrid—every animal in the train — have raised head and pricked up ears, with nostrils distended. Even the horned cattle to rearward have caught the infection, and low loudly in response to the neighing of the horses and the hinneying of the mules. There is a very *fracas* of noises, like a Bedlam broke loose, the voice of the *mayor-domo* rising above all as he cries out,

"*Guarda, la estampeda !*"

And a "stampede" it becomes, all knowing the cause. The animals have scented water, and no longer need whip-lash or cry to urge them on. Instead, teamsters and *arrieros* find it impossible to restrain them, for it were a struggle against Nature itself. Taking the bits between their teeth, and regardless of rein, horses, mules, all rush simultaneously and madly forward, as if each had a score of gad-flies with their venomous probosces buried deep in its body.

A helter-skelter it is, with a loud hullabulloo, the heavily-laden wagons drawn over the ground as light-like and with the velocity of bicycles, and making noise as of thunder. For now, near the mountain's foot, the plain is bestrewed with stones, some big enough to raise the wheels on high, almost to overturning the vehicles, eliciting agonized cries from the women and children inside them. No more are Indians thought of for the time; enough danger without that, from upsets, broken bones, indeed death.

In the end none of these eventualites arise. Luckily—and more by good luck than guiding—-the wagons keep their balance, and they within them their places, till all come to a stand again. While still tearing on, they see before them a disc of water lit up by the last rays of departing sunlight, with half a dozen horsemen—the reconnoitring party—drawn up on its edge, in attitude of wonder at their coming after so soon.

But their animals, still in rush, give no opportunity for explanation. On go they into the lake, horses, mules, and cattle mingled together; nor stop till they are belly deep, with the water up over their nostrils. No more neighing nor lowing now, but all silent, swilling, and contented.

CHAPTER IV.

EL OJO DE AGUA.

MORNING dawns upon the Lost Mountain, to disclose a scene such as had never before been witnessed in that solitary spot. For never before had wagon, or other wheeled vehicle, approached it. Remote from town or civilized settlement, leagues away from any of the customary routes of travel, the only white men having occasion to visit it had been hunters or gold-seekers, and their visits, like those of angels, few and far between. Red men, however, have sought it more frequently, for it is not far from one of their great war-trails—that leading from the Apache country to the settlements on the Horcasitas, so serving these savages as a convenient halting-place when on raid thither. The reconnoitring party, sent in advance of the caravan, had discovered traces of their presence by the lake's edge; but none recent, and nothing to signify. There were no fresh tracks upon the meadow-grass, nor the belt of naked sand around the water, save those of wild animals that had come thither to quench their thirst.

In confidence, therefore, the miners made camp, though not negligently or carelessly. The old *militario* had seen too much campaigning for that, and directed the wagons to be drawn up in a *corral* of oval shape, tongues and tails united as the links of a chain. Long-bodied vehicles, the six enclose a considerable space—enough to accommodate all who have need to stay inside. In case of attack it could be still further strengthened by the bales, boxes, and *alparejas* of the pack-mules. Outside the animals were staked, and are still upon their tethers, though without much concern about their running away. After the long traverse over the dry *llanos*, and the suffering they have endured, now on such good grass, and beside such sweet water, they will contentedly stay till it please their masters to remove them.

Fires had been kindled the night before, but only for cooking supper; it is summer, and there is no discomfort from cold — heat rather. And now at dawn the fires are being re-lighted with a view to *desayuna*, and later on breakfast; for, though the caravan had unexpectedly run short of water, its stock of provisions is still unexhausted.

Among the earliest up—nay, the very first— is Pedro Vicente. Not with any intention to take part in culinary operations. *Gambusino* and guide, he would scorn such menial occupations. His reasons for being so early astir are altogether different and twofold ; though but one of them has he made known, and that only to Henry Tresillian. Overnight, ere retiring to rest, he had signified his intention to ascend the Cerro in the morning — soon as there was enough of daylight to make the ascent practicable—in hopes of finding game both of the furred and feathered sorts, he said. For in addition to his *métier* as guide to the caravan— being a skilled hunter as well as gold-seeker— he holds engagement to supply it with venison, or such other meat commodity as may fall to his gun. For days he has had but little opportunity of showing his hunter skill. On the sterile tract through which they have been passing birds and quadrupeds are scarce, even such as usually inhabit it having gone elsewhere in consequence of the long-continued drought. All the more is he desirous to make up for late deficit, and at least furnish the table of the quality with something fresh. He knows there are game animals on the mountain — a *mesa*, as already said, level-topped, with trees growing over it, besides water; for there is the fountain's head, source of the stream and lake below On the night before, he had spoken of wild sheep as likely to be found above, with antelopes, and possibly a bear or two, also turkeys. Now, in the morning, he is sure about these last, having heard them, as is their wont before sunrise, saluting one another with that sonorous call from which they derive their Mexican name, *guajaloté.*

These confidences he has imparted to Henry Tresillian, who is to accompany him in the chase, though not from any view of inspiring the latter with its ardour. There is no need; the young Englishman being a hunter by instinct, with a love for natural history as well, and the Lost Mountain promises rich reward for the climbing, in discovery as in sport. Besides, the two have been *compagnons de chasse* all along the route; habitually together, the fellow-feeling of huntership making such association congenial. So, early as is the Mexican afoot, he beats the English youth by barely a minute of time; the latter seen issuing forth from one of the tents that form part of the encampment, just as the former has crawled out from between the wheels of a wagon, under which, rolled up in his *frezada*, he had passed the night.

With just enough light to identify him,
Henry Tresillian is seen to be habited in
shooting coat, breeches, and gaiters, laced
buskins, and a tweed cloth cap; in short, the
costume of an English sportsman — shot-belt
over the shoulders, and double-barrel in hand
—about to attack a pheasant preserve, or go
tramping through stubble and swedes. The
gambusino himself wears the picturesque
dress of his class and country; the gun he
carries being a rifle, while the sword-like
weapon hanging along his hip is the ever-
present *macheté*—in Sonora sometimes called
cortanté.

As, overnight, the programme had been all
arranged, their interchange of speech at present
has only reference to something in the way of
desayuna before setting out. This they find
ready and near; at the central camp fire now
blazing up, where several of the women,
"whisks" in hand, are bending over pots of
chocolate, stirring the substantial liquid to a
creamy froth.

A *taza* of it is handed to each of the "*caza-dores*," with a "*tortilla enchilada*," accompanied by a graceful word of welcome. Then, empty-ing the cups, and chewing up the tough, leather-like maize cakes, the hunters slip quietly out of camp, and set their faces for the Cerro.

The ascent, commenced almost immediately, is by a ravine — a sort of gorge or chine worn out by the water from the spring-head above and disintegrating rains throughout the long ages. They find it steep as a staircase, though not winding as one; instead, trending straight up from its debouchment on the plain to the summit level, between slopes, these with grim, rocky *façade*, still more precipitous. Down its bottom cascades the stream—a tiny rivulet now, but in rain-storms a torrent — and along this lies the path, the only one by which the Cerro can be ascended, as the *gambusino* already knows.

"There's no other," he says, as they are clambering upward, "where a man could make the ascent, unless with a Jacob's ladder let down to him. All around, the cliff is as steep as the shaft of a mine. Even the wild sheep can't scale it, and if we find any on the summit — and it's to be hoped we shall — they must either have been bred there, or gone up this way. *Guarda!*" he adds, in exclamation, as he sees the impulsive English youth bounding on rather recklessly. " Have a care! Don't disturb the stones ; they may go rattling down and smash somebody below."

" By Jove! I didn't think of that," returns he thus cautioned, turning pale at thought of how he might have endangered the lives of those dear to him; then ascending more slowly, and with the care enjoined upon him.

In due time they arrive at the head of the gorge, there stopping to take breath. Only for an instant, when they proceed on, now no longer in a climb, the path thence leading over ground level as the plain itself; but still by the rivulet's edge, through a tangle of trees and bushes.

At some two hundred yards from the head

of the gorge they come into an opening, the
Mexican as he enters it exclaiming,

"*El ojo de agua!*"

CHAPTER V.

THE phrase, "*ojo de agua*" (the water's eye), is simply the Mexican name for a spring; which Henry Tresillian needs not to be told, being already acquainted with the pretty poetical appellation. And he now sees the thing itself but a few paces ahead, gurgling up in a little circular basin, and sending off the stream which supplies the lake below.

In an instant they are upon its edge, to find it clear as crystal, the *gambusino* saying, as he unslings his drinking-cup of cow's horn,

" I can't resist taking a swill of it, notwithstanding the gallons I had swallowed overnight. After such a long spell of short-water rations, one feels as though he could never again get enough." Then filling the horn, and almost

41

instantly emptying it, he concludes with the
exclamation "*Delicioso!*"

His companion drinks also, but from a cup
of solid silver; vessels of this metal, even of
gold, being aught but rare among the master-
miners of Sonora.

They are about to continue on, when lo! a
flock of large birds by the edge of the open.
On the ground these are—having just come
out from among the bushes—moving leisurely
along, with beaks now and then lowered to the
earth; in short, feeding as turkeys in a pasture
field.   And turkeys they are, the Mexican
saying in a whisper,

"*Los guajalotes!*"

So like are they to the domestic bird—only
better shaped and every way more beautiful—
that Henry Tresillian has no difficulty in identifying them as its wild progenitors.   One of
superior size, an old cock, is at their head, stri-
ding to and fro in all the pride of his glittering
plumage, which, under the beams of the new-
risen sun, shows hues vivid and varied as those

of the rainbow. A very sultan he seems, followed by a train of sultanas and their attendants; for there are young birds in the flock, fledglings, that differ in appearance from the old ones.

Suddenly the grand satrap erects his head, and with neck craned out, utters a note of alarm. Too late. " Bang—bang !" from the double-barrel — the sharper crack of the rifle sounding simultaneously—and the old cock, with three of his satellites, lies prostrate upon the earth, the rest taking flight with terrified screeches, and a clatter of wings loud as the " whirr" of a threshing machine.

" Not a bad beginning," quietly observes the *gambusino*, as they stand over the fallen game. " Is it, señorito ? "

"Anything but that," answers the young Englishman, delighted at having secured such a good bottom for their bag. " But what are we to do with them ? We can't carry them along."

" Certainly not," rejoins the Mexican. " Nor need. Let them lie where they are till we

come back. But no," he adds, correcting himself. " That will never do. There are wolves
up here, no doubt — certainly coyotes, if no
other kind—and on return we might find only
feathers. So we must string them up out of
reach."

The stringing up is a matter which occupies
only a few minutes' time; done by one leg
thrust through the opened sinew of the other
to form a loop; then the birds hoisted aloft,
and hung upon the up-curving arms of a tall
pitahaya.

"And now, on !" says the *gambusino*, after
re-loading guns. " Let us hope we may come
across something in the four-legged line, big
enough to give everybody a bit of fresh meat
for dinner. Likely we'll have to tramp a good
way before sighting any ; the report of our
guns will have frighted both birds and beasts,
and sent all to the farthest side of the *mesa.*
But no matter for that. I want to go there
direct, and at once, for a reason, *muchacho,*
I 've not yet made known to you."

While speaking, an anxious expression has shown itself on the *gambusino's* face, which, taken in connection with his last words, leads Henry Tresillian to suspect something in, or on, his mind, beside the desire to kill game. Moreover, before leaving the camp he had noticed that the Mexican seemed to act in a manner more excited than was his wont—as if in a great hurry to get away. That, no doubt, for the reason he now hints at; though what it is the young Englishman cannot even give a guess.

"May I know it now?" he asks, with some eagerness, noting the grave look.

"Certainly you may, and shall," frankly responds the Mexican. "I would have told you sooner, and the others as well, but for not being sure about it. I didn't like to cause an alarm in the camp without good reason. And I hope still there's none. After all it may not have been smoke."

"Smoke! What?"

"What I saw, or thought I saw, yesterday

evening, just after we arrived by the lake's edge."

" Where ? "

" To the north-east—a long way off."

" But if it was a smoke, what would that signify ? "

" In this part of the world, much. It might mean danger; ay, death."

" You astonish—mystify me, Senor Vicente. How could it mean that?"

" There 's no mystery in it, *muchacho.* Where smoke is seen there should be fire; and a fire on these *llanos* is likely to be one with Indians around it. Now do you understand the danger I 'm thinking of ? "

" I do. But I thought there were no Indians in this part of the country, except the Opatas; and they are Christianized, dwelling in towns."

" True, all that. But the Opata towns are far from here, and in an entirely different direction—the very opposite. If smoke it was, the fire that made it wasn't one kindled by

Opatas, but men who only resemble them in the colour of their skin—Indians, too."

"What Indians do you suspect?"

"*Los Apaches.*"

"Danger indeed, if they be in the neighbourhood." The young Englishman has been long enough in Sonora to have acquaintance with the character of these cruel savages. "But I hope they're not," he adds, trustfully, still with some apprehension, as his thoughts turn to those below.

"That hope I heartily echo," rejoins the Mexican, "for if they be about, we've got to look out for the skin of our heads. But come, *muchacho mio!* Don't let us be down in the mouth till we're sure there *is* a danger. As I've said, I'm not even sure of having seen smoke at all. It might have been a dust-whirl. just as I noticed the thing, the *estampeda* commenced; and after it the rush for water, which of course took off my attention. When that was over, and I again turned my eyes north-eastward, it was too dark to distinguish smoke or anything else. I then looked for a light all along the sky-line, and also several times during the night—luckily to see none. For all I can't help having fears. A man who's once been prisoner to the Apaches never travels through a district where they are like to be encountered without some apprehension. Mine ought to be of the keenest. I've not only been their prisoner, but rather roughly handled, as no doubt you'll admit after looking at this."

Saying which, the Mexican opens his shirt-front, laying bare his breast; on which appears a disc, bearing rude resemblance to a "death's head," burnt deep into the skin.

"They gave me that brand," he continues, "just by way of amusing themselves. They meant to have further diversion out of it by using me as a target, and it for a centre mark at one of their shooting matches. Luckily, before that came off, I found the chance of giving them leg-bail. Now, *muchacho*, you'll better understand my anxiety to be up here so early, and why I want to push on to the other end. *Vamonos!*"

Shouldering their guns, they proceed onward; now at slower pace, their progress obstructed by thick-growing bushes and trees, with *llianas* interlacing. For beyond the spring there is neither stream nor path, save here and there a slight trace, often tortuous, which tells of the passage of wild animals wandering to and fro. The hunters are pleased to see it thus; still more when the Mexican, noting some hoof-marks in a spot of soft ground, pronounces them tracks of the *carnero cimmaron.*

"I thought we'd find some of the big-horn gentry up here," he says; "and if all the caravan don't this day dine on roast mutton, it'll be because Pedro Vicente isn't the proper man to be its purveyor. Still, we mustn't stop to go after the sheep now. True, we've begun the day hunting, but before proceeding farther with that, we must make sure we shan't have to end it fighting. Ssh!"

The sibillatory exclamation has reference to

a noise heard a little way off, like the stroke of a hoof upon hard turf, several times rapidly repeated. And simultaneous with it another sound, as the snort or bark of some animal.

"That's a *carnero*, now!" says the Mexican, *sotto voce;* as he speaks, coming to a stop and laying hold of the other's arm to restrain him. "Since the game offers itself without going after, or out of our way, we may as well secure a head or two. Like the turkeys, it can be strung up till our return."

Of course his *compagnon de chasse* is of the same mind. He but longs to empty his double-barrel again, all the more at such grand game, and rejoins, saying, "Just so; it can."

Without further speech they stalk cautiously forward, to reach the edge of another opening, and there behold another flock—not of birds, but quadrupeds. Deer they might seem at the first glance, to eyes unacquainted with them; and for such Henry Tresillian might mistake them, but that they show no antlers; instead, horns of a character proclaiming them sheep.

Sheep they are, wild ones, different from the domesticated animal as greyhound from dacshund. No short legs nor low bodies theirs; no bushy tails, nor tangle of wool to encumber them. Instead, coats clean and smooth, with limbs long, sinewy, and supple as those of stag itself. Several pairs of horns are visible in the flock, one pair spirally curving much larger than any of the others; indeed, of such dimensions, and seeming weight, as to make it a wonder how the old ram, their owners, can hold up his head. Yet is it he who is holding head highest; the same who had snorted, hammering the ground with his hoof.

He has done so, repeatedly, since; the last time to be the last in his life. Through the leafy branches, cautiously parted, shoots out a double jet of flame and smoke; three cracks are heard; then again there is dead game on the ground.

This time, however, counting less in heads; only one—that carrying the grand curvature of horns. Alone the leader of the flock has fallen

4—2

to the second fusillade, killed by the rifle's
bullet. For the shot from the double-barrel,
though hitting too, has glanced off the thick
felt-like coats of the *carneros* as from a corslet
of steel.

"*Carrai!*" exclaims the *gambusino*, with a
vexed air, as they step up to the fallen quarry.
"This time we haven't done so well—in fact,
worse than nothing."

"But why?" queries the young Englishman,
in wonder at the other's strange words and
ways, after having made such a big kill.

"Why, you ask, señorito! Don't . your
nostrils tell you? *Mil diablos!* how the brute
stinks!"

Truth he speaks, as his hunting companion,
now standing over the dead body of the big-
horn, can well perceive—sensible of an offensive
odour arising from it as that of ram in the
rutting season.

"What a fool I've been to spend bullet
upon him!" continues the Mexican, without
awaiting rejoinder. "Nor was it his great

bulk or horns that tempted me. No; all through thinking of that other thing, which made me careless which of them I aimed at."

"What other thing?"

"The smoke. Well, it's no use crying over spilt milk nor any to bother more about the brute. It's only fit food for coyotes; and the sooner they get it into their bellies the better. Faugh! Let us away from it."

CHAPTER VI

A HOMERIC REPAST.

EARLY as are the white men astir, yet earlier are the red ones. For the Coyoteros, like the animal from which they derive their tribal name, do more of their prowling by night than by day. Moreover, it is the sultry season, and they design reaching Nauchampa-tepetl before the sun gets so high and hot as to make travelling uncomfortable. Even savages are not averse to comfort; though these are now thinking more about that of their horses than their own. They are on an expedition that will need keeping the animals up to their best strength ; and journeying in the noon hours would distress and pull them down.

So nearly an hour before dawn declines itself they are up and active, moving about in the dim light, silent as spectres. Silent, not from any fear of betraying their presence to an enemy—they know of none likely to be near—but because it is their habit.

What they first do is to shift the picket-pins of their horses, or give greater length to the trail-ropes, in order that the animals may get a bite of clean fresh grass, that on which they were tethered throughout the night being now trampled down.

Next, they proceed to take care of themselves —to fortify the inner man with a bit of breakfast. No fire is needed for the cooking it, and none is kindled. The *mezcal* and horse-meat pie has been baking all the night; and now, near morning, they know it will be ready—done to a turn. It but needs the turf lifted off their primitive oven, and the contents extracted.

Five or six, detailed for the task, at once set about it; first taking off the top sods, now calcined and still smoking. Then the loose mould, which the fire has converted into ashes, is removed with more care. It is hot, and needs handling gingerly ; but the savage *cuisi-niers* know how, and soon the black bundle is exposed to view, the hide now hairless and charred, but moist and reeking. It still adheres sufficiently to bear hoisting out, without fear of spilling the contents ; and at length it is so lifted and carried to a clean spot of sward. Then cut open and spread out, there is displayed a steaming savoury mass, whose appetizing odour, borne upward and outward on the fresh morning air, inspires every red-skin around with delightful anticipations.

And not without reason either. To say nothing of the baked horseflesh—by many *gourmets* esteemed a delectable dish—the corn of the *mezcal*, treated thus, is a viand palatable as peculiar. And peculiar it is, bearing resemblance to nothing I either know or can think of. In appearance it is much like candied citron, with a sweetish taste too, only firmer and darker in colour. But while eating it the tongue seems penetrated with a thousand tiny darts ; a sort of prinkling sensation, quite indescribable, and, to one unaccustomed to it, not altogether agreeable. In time this passes away; and he who has made the experiment of eating *mezcal* comes to like it exceedingly. Many grand people among the whites regard it in the light of a luxury; and as such it has found its way into most Mexican towns—even the capital itself — where it commands a high price.

With the Apache Indians, as already said, it is a staple food, even giving their tribal name to one branch of this numerous nation—the Mezcaleros. But all eat of it alike, and the Coyoteros, *en bivouac*, show, by their knowledge of how to prepare it, that baked *mezcal* is noways new to them.

At the word "ready!" they gather around the hot steaming mass; and, regardless of scorched lips or tongues, set upon it with knife and tooth.

Soon the skin is cleaned out, every scrap of its contents eaten. They could eat the hide too, and would, were there a pinch. But there

is none such now, and it is left for their name-
sakes, the coyotes.

A smoke follows the Homeric repast, for all
American Indians are addicted to the use of
the nicotian weed. They were so before the
caravels of Columbus spread sail on the Haytian
seas.

Every Coyotero in camp has his pipe and
pouch of tobacco, be it genuine or adulterated ;
this depending on how their luck has been
running, or how recent their latest raid upon
some settlement of the pale-faces.

Pipes smoked out and returned to their
places of deposit, all are afoot again. Nothing
more now but to draw picket-pins, coil up trail-
ropes, mount, and move off; for their horse
caparison, scant and easily adjusted, is already
on.

The chief gives the order "to horse," not
in words, but by example—springing upon the
back of his own. Then they ride off, as before,
in formation "by twos," each file falling into
rank as the line lengthens out upon the plain.

Scarce is the last file clear of the abandoned camp-ground ere this becomes occupied by animated beings of another kind — wolves, whose howling has been heard throughout all the night. Having scented the slaughtered horse, these now rush simultaneously towards it, to dispute the banquet of bones.

*   *   *   *   *

Shortly after leaving the camp the marching red-skins lose sight of the Cerro. This is accounted for by a dip in the plain, with a ridge-like swell beyond, which runs transversely to their course.. The hollow continues for several miles before the mountain will be again in view; but, well knowing the way, they need not this to guide them. Nor are they in any particular hurry. They can reach their intended halting-place by the lake long ere the sun becomes sultry, there to lie up till the cool hours of evening. So they move leisurely along, and with a purpose—to spare the sinews of their horses.

They talk enough now, loudly and laugh-

ingly. They have slept well, and breakfasted
satisfactorily; besides, it is broad daylight, and
no danger to be apprehended, no fear of hostile
surprise. For all that they keep their eyes on
the alert through habitude, every now and
then scanning the horizon around.

Soon they see that which gives them something serious to speak about. Not upon the
horizon, nor anywhere upon the plain, but up
in the heavens above it — birds. What of
them? And what in their appearance to attract
the attention of the Coyoteros? Nothing, or
not much, were the birds other than they are.
But they are vultures, black vultures of two
sorts — *gallinazos* and *zopilotes*. Nor would
the Indians think of giving them a second
glance were they soaring about in their ordinary way, wheeling in circles and spirals.
But they are not; instead, passing overhead
in straight onward flight, with a quick, earnest
plying of wings, evidently making for some
point where they expect to stoop upon carrion.
Scores there are of them, straggled out in a

long stream, but all flying in one direction—
the same in which the savages are themselves
proceeding—towards Nauchampa-tepetl.

What can be drawing the vultures thither?
This the question which the Indians ask one
another, in their own formularies of speech;
none able to answer it, save by conjecture.
Without in any way alarming, the spectacle
excites them; and they quicken their pace,
eager to learn what is attracting the birds.
It should be something more than dead antelope or deer, so many are tending towards it,
and from so far. For their high flight, straight
onward, tells of their having been for some
time keeping the same course.

Hastening on up the slope of the swell, the
dusky horsemen once more catch sight of the
mountain, there to see what brings them to
an abrupt halt—a filmy purplish haze hanging
over its southern end, more scattered higher
up in the sky. Is it fog rising from the water
they know to be there? No: smoke, as their
practised eyes tell them after regarding it a

moment.   And with like celerity they interpret it, as proceeding from the fire, or fires,
of a camp.   Other travellers, anticipating them,
are encamped by Nauchampa-tepetl,

Who?   Opatas?   Not likely.   Sons of toil
—*Indicos mansos*—slaves, as these the *bravos*,
their kindred only in race, scornfully call them
—the Opatas keep to their towns, and the
patches of cultivation around them.   Improbable
that they should have ventured into that wilderness so far from home.   More likely it is a
party of pale-faces; men in seach of that shining
metal which, as the Apaches know, has often
lured their white enemies into the very heart of
the desert, their own domain, and to destruction
—themselves the destroyers.   If the smoke of
those camp fires they now see be over such a
party, then is it doomed—at least so mentally
resolve the red centaurs, hoping it may be thus.

While still gazing at the blue cloud, taking its
measure, and discussing the probabilities of who
and what sort of men may be under it, another
appears before their eyes ; this whiter and of

smaller size—a mere puff suddenly rising over the crest of the *mesa*, and separating from it as it drifts higher.

From the fire of a gun, or guns, as the Coyoteros can tell, though not by any crack of one having reached their ears, since none has. In the rarefied atmosphere of the high-lying *llanos* the eye has the advantage of the ear, sounds being heard only at short distance. They are still more than ten miles from the mountain, and the report of a cannon, discharged on its summit, would be barely audible to them.

Still staying at halt, but keeping to their horses, the chief and others in authority enter into consultation. And while they are deliberating on the best course to be pursued, still another puff of smoke shoots up over the *mesa*, similar to that preceding, but at a different point. It aids them in coming to conclusions; for now they are sure there is a camp of palefaces by the pond ; and they above are hunters who have gone up to get game, which the Indians know to be there in abundance.

But what sort of pale-faces? Of this they
are not sure. Knowing it to be a miners' camp,
they would ride straight on for it, in gallop.
But it may be an encampment of *soldados*, which
would make a difference. Not that the Coyoteros are afraid to encounter Mexican soldiers
—far from it. Rather would they rejoice at
finding it these. For their tribe, their own
branch of it, has an old score against the men
in uniform; and nothing would please them
better than an oportunity to settle it. Indeed,
partly to seek this, with purposes of plunder
combined, are they now on the *war trail.* Only
in their mode of action would there be a difference, in the event of the encampment turning
out to be occupied by *soldados.* Soldiers in that
quarter should be cavalry, and to approach them
caution would be called for, with strategy. But
these red centaurs are soldiers themselves—
veterans, skilled, cunning strategists—and now
give proof of it. For the time has come for
them to advance ; which they do, not straight
forward nor in single body, but broken into two

bands, one facing right, the other left, with a design to enfilade the camp by approaching it from opposite points. Separating at the start, the two cohorts soon diverge wide apart, both making for the mountain, but with the intention to reach its southern end on different sides.

If the black vultures, still in streaming flight above, have hopes of getting a repast there, they may now feel assured of its being a plenteous one.

CHAPTER VII.

LOS INDIOS!

PARTING from the despised carcase of the ram the hunters press onward, the younger with mental resolve to return to it, come back what way they will. Its grand spiral horns have caught his fancy: such a pair would grace any hall in Christendom; and, though he cannot call the trophy his own, since it fell not to his gun, he intends appropriating it.

Only for a brief moment does the young Englishman reflect about them; in the next they are out of his mind. For, glancing at the Mexican's face, he again sees that look of anxious uneasiness noted before. It had returned soon as the exciting incident of the sheep-shooting was over. And knowing the cause, he shares it; no more thinking about the chase or its trophies.

They say but little now, having sufficient work to occupy them without wasting time in words. For beyond the opening where the *carneros* were encountered, they find no path —not so much as a trace made by animals— and have to make one for themselves. As the trees stand close, with *llanas* interlacing, the Mexican is often compelled to use his *machete* for hewing out a passage-way; which he does with an accompaniment of *carrambas!* thick as the underwood he chops at.

Thus impeded, they are nearly an hour in getting through the *chapparal*, though the distance passed is less than the half of a mile. But at length they accomplish it, arriving on the *mesa's* outer edge, close to that of the cliff. There the tall timber ends in a skirting of low bushes, and their view is no longer obstructed. North, east, and west the *llano* is under their eyes to the horizon's verge, twenty miles at least being within the scope of their vision.

They aim not to scan it so far. For at a
distance of little more than ten they observe
that which at once fixes their glance : a dun
yellowish disc—a cloud—with its base resting
upon the plain.

"Smoke, no—but dust !" exclaims the *gambusino,* soon as sighting it; "and kicked up
by the heels of horses—hundreds of them.
There can be nothing else out there to cause
that. Horses with men on their backs. If a
caballada of wild mustangs, the dust would
show more scattered. *Indios, por cierto !
Carra-i !"* he says in continuation, the shade
on his brow sensibly darkening, as with a quick
glance over his shoulder he sees real smoke in
that direction. "What fools we've been to
kindle fires ! Rank madness. Better to have
eaten breakfast raw. I myself most to blame
of any ; I should have known the danger. By
this they'll have spied our camp smoke—that
of our shots, too. Ah, *muchacho !* we've been
foolish in every way."

Almost breathless from this burst of regret

and self-recrimination, he is for a while silent;
his heart beating audibly, however, as with gaze
fixed on the far-off cloud, he endeavours to
interpret it. But the dark cloud soon becomes
less dense, partially dispersed, and under it
appears something more solid; a clump of
sombre hue, but with here and there sparkling
points. No separate forms can as yet be
made out; only a mass; but for all that, the
gambusino knows it to be composed of horses
and men, the corruscations being the glint of
arms and accoutrements, as the sun penetrates
through to them.

"What a pity," he exclaims, resuming speech,
"I didn't think of asking Don Estevan for the
loan of his telescope! If we only had it here
now! But I can see enough without it; 't is
as I feared. No more hunting for us to-day;
but fighting ere the sun goes down—perhaps
ere it reach meridian. *Mira!* the thing's
splitting into two. You see, señorito?"

The señorito does see that the dust-cloud
has parted in twain, as also the dark mass

underneath. And now they can distinguish separate forms; horses with men on their backs, and a more conspicuous glittering of arms, because of their being in motion.

"Ah, yes!" adds the Mexican, with increased gravity of tone, "*Indios bravos* they are, hundreds of them. If Apaches, as sure they must, Heaven help us all! I know what they mean by that movement. They've sighted the camp smoke, and intend coming on along both sides of the Cerro. That's why they've broken into two bands. Back to camp, as fast as our legs can carry us! We've not a minute—not a second—to lose. *Vamos!*"

And back for camp they start, not to spend time on the way as when coming from it, but in a run and rush along the path already opened—past the dead sheep, past the spring, and the strung-up turkeys, without even staying to look at these, much less think of taking them along.

* * * * *

The occupants of the miners' camp, men,

women, and children, are up and active now. Some are at work about the wagons, pouring water over their wheels to tighten the tires, loose from the shrinking of the wood; others have set to mending harness and pack-saddles; while still others, out on the open plain, are changing the animals to fresh spots of pasturage. A small party is seen around the carcase of a bullock, in the act of skinning it to get beefsteaks for breakfast.

Several fires have been kindled, for the people are many, and have separate messes, according to rank and vocation. Around these are the women and grown girls, some bending over red earthenware pots that contain choco· late and coffee, others on their knees with the *metate* stone in front, and *metlapilla* in hand, crushing the boiled maize into paste for the indispensable *tortillas*. The children play by the lake's edge, wading ankle-deep into the water, plashing about like little ducks; some of the bigger boys, who have improvised a rude tackle, endeavouring to catch fish. In

this remote tarn there are such, as it has an
affluent stream connecting it with the Rio
Horcasitas—now nearly dry, but at times having
a volume of water sufficient for the finny tribes
to ascend to the lake, into which several species
have found their way.

Within the space enclosed by the wagons—
the *corral*—three tents have been erected, and
stand in a row. The middle one is a large
square marquee, the two flanking it of the
ordinary bell shape. The marquee is occupied
by the senior partner and his señora; the one,
on the right by their daughter and an Indian
moza — her waiting-maid; the third affords
shelter and sleeping quarters for the two
Tresillians.

All three are for a time empty, their occupants having stepped out of them. As known,
Henry Tresillian has gone up to the summit of
the Cerro, and his father is moving about the
camp in the company of the *mayor-domo*, with
an eye to superintendence of everything; while
Don Estevan, his wife, and daughter, have

strolled out along the lake's edge to enjoy the refreshing breeze wafted over its water. The three promenaders have but made one turn along the sandy shore, and back again, when they hear a cry which not only alarms them, but all within and around the camp.—

"*Los Indios!*"

It has been sent from above—from the head of the ravine; and everybody looks up—all eyes raised simultaneously. To see two men standing on a projecting point of rock, their figures sharply outlined against the blue background of sky; at the same time to recognize them as the *gambusino* and Henry Tresillian. Only for an instant are these at a stand; only to shout down those terrible words of warning; then both bound into the gorge, and come on at a rush, with risk of breaking their necks.

At its bottom they are met by an excited, clamorous crowd; surrounded and assailed by a very tempest of interrogations. But to these they vouchsafe no answer beyond that implied

in their shout ; instead, push on to where Don
Estevan and the elder Tresillian, now together,
stand awaiting them. The senior partner is the
first to speak, addressing himself to Vicente :

"You've seen Indians, Don Pedro? Where?"

"Out upon the *llano*, your worship—to north-
eastward."

" You're sure of it being Indians ?"

" Quite sure, señor. We were able to make
horses with men on them ; the men unlike any
with a white skin, but just as those with a red
one. Your worship can take my word for their
being Indians."

" I can, and do. But from what you say, it
seems they're still a good way off. How far,
think you ?"

" Ten miles or more, when we came away
from the place where we saw them. They
can't be much nearer yet, as we've not been
over ten minutes on the way."

The quick time made by the hunters in
return is attested by their breathing ; both with
nostrils agape and breasts heaving up and

down as runners at the close of a hard-con-
tested race.

"'T is well they're at such a distance," rejoins Don Estevan. "And lucky your having
sighted them before they got nearer."

"Ah! señor, they'll soon be near; for I
know they've sighted us—at least the smoke
of our camp, and are already making for it.
Light horsemen as they don't need long to
traverse ten miles—on a plain like this."

"That's true," assents the *ci-devant* soldier,
with an air of troubled impatience. "What
do you advise our doing, Don Pedro?"

"Well, for one thing, your worship, we
mustn't remain here. We must clear out of
this camp as soon as possible. In an hour—
ay, less—it may be too late."

"Your words want explaining, Don Pedro.
I don't comprehend them. Clear out of the
camp! But whither are we to go?"

"*Arriba!*" answers the guide, pointing to
the gorge, "up yonder."

"But we can't take the animals there. And

to carry up our goods there wouldn't be time."

" I know it, your worship. And glad we may be to get ourselves safe up."

" Then we're to abandon all ? Is that what you advise ? "

" It is. I'm sorry I can give no better advice. There's no alternative if we wish to live."

" To lose everything," puts in the junior partner, "goods, animals, machinery ! That would be a terrible calamity. Surely, Señor Vicente, we can defend the camp; our people are all well armed."

" Impossible, Don Roberto; impossible were they ever so well armed. From what I could make out of the Indian party it numbers hundreds to our tens, sufficient of them to surround us on every side. And even if we could keep them off during daylight, at night they'd crawl close enough to set the camp on fire. Wagons, tilts, every stick and stitch of them are dry as tinder; the very pack-saddles would be ablaze with the first spark that fell on them "

"But how know we that these Indians are hostile? After all, it may be some friendly band; perhaps Opatas?"

"No!" exclaims the *gambusino* impatiently. "I saw enough to know they're not Opatas, nor *mansos* of any kind; enough to be sure they're *bravos*, and almost sure, Apaches."

"Apaches!" echo several voices in the surrounding, in tones proclaiming the dread with which this name inspires the heart of every Sonoreno. Every man present feels a creeping sensation in the skin of his head, as though the scalping-knife were being brandished around it.

"They're coming from the direction where Apaches would come," pursues Vicente. "Besides, they have no baggage; not a woman or child to be seen with them. All men, mounted and armed."

"Indeed, if it be so," rejoins Don Estevan, with brow now darkly shadowed, "we can expect no friendship from them."

"No mercy either!" adds the gold-seeker. "Nor have we a right to expect it, after the

treatment they've had at the hands of Captain
Gil Perez and his men."

All know to what Vicente alludes: a massacre of Apache Indians by a party of Mexican
soldiers, after being lured and lulled into fase
security by professions of peace—cold-blooded
and cruel, as any recorded in the annals of
frontier warfare.

"I've said it. I'm good as sure they're
Apaches," repeats the *gambusino*, more impres-
sively. "And it would be madness, sheer
insanity, to await them here. We must up to
the *mesa*."

"But will we be safe there?"

"As in a citadel. No fortress ever contrived,
or made by hand of man, is strong as the
Cerro Perdido. Twenty men could hold it
against as many hundreds — ay, thousands.
Carramba! We may thank the Virgin for
providing us with such a secure retreat; so
handy, and just in the nick of time."

"Then let us to it," assents Don Estevan,
after a brief consultation with his partner, who

no longer opposes the step, though by it they may lose their all. "We'll follow your advice, Señor Vicente; and you have our authority to order everything as it seems best to you."

"I've only one order to give, your worships; that's *arriba!* Up, all and everybody!"

CHAPTER VIII.

THE excitement in the camp, already at full height, now changes to a quick, confused hurrying to and fro, accompanied by cries of many kinds. Here and there is heard the terrified scream of a woman, who, babe in arms, fancies the spear of a savage pointed at her breast, to impale herself and offspring.

There is a rush for the gorge, up which a stream of human forms is soon seen swarming as ants up their hill. And, with a gallantry which distinguishes the miner as the mariner, the women and children are permitted foremost place in the upward retreat, assisted by husbands.

Without serious accident all succeed in reaching the summit, where the women are left, the

80

men who went with them hurrying back below.
It is hard to part with valuable property and
cherished household gods—still harder to see
these appropriated by a hated enemy—and an
effort is to be made for saving what can be
saved. At first they only thought of their
lives; but half a dozen men, who had sprung
to their horses at the earliest moment of alarm,
and galloped out beyond the mountain's flank
to get better view, signal back that the Indians
are not yet in sight. So there is still a chance
to take up a portion of the camp equipage, with
such goods as are likely to be most needed in
the event of their having to sustain a siege.

" The ammunition and provender first!" shouts
Vicente, back again at camp, with full authority
of direction. " Take up everything that's food
for man and loading for gun. After that whatever we'll have time for."

Knowing their women now safe, the men
work with spirit; and soon a different sort of
stream is seen ascending the gorge: a string
of burden-bearers, continuous from plain to

6

summit; hastily returning down again, relieved
of their loads, to take up others. Never were
bees so busy. Some remain below, getting the
goods out of the wagons, and making packages
of them, convenient for the difficult transport.
The bales and boxes—lading of the pack-mules
—are broken open, and their more valuable
effects picked out and carried off; so that in a
short space of time not much remains save the
mining tools and machinery, with the heavier
articles of house furniture.

Could the Rattlesnake have known of this
quick precautionary sacking of the camp by its
owners, he and his would have approached it
in greater haste. But they are seen coming on
now. The mounted videttes have at length
signalled them in sight, they themselves galloping in at the same time, and dropping down
from their horses.

There is a last gathering up of bundles, which
includes the two smaller tents — the marquee
left standing. Then the final *debandade;* all
turning face towards the gorge, and toiling up it.

No, not all as yet; more than one lingers below. For the horses must needs be left behind; impossible to take them up a steep where only goat, sheep, or clawed creature might go. And more than one has a master who parts with it reluctantly. Regretfully, too, at thought of its changing owner, and to such owner as will soon enter upon possession. Even some of the teamsters and muleteers have an affection for their mules, the head *arriero* regarding the whole *atajo* as his children, and the "bell-mare" almost as a mother. Many a long mile and league has he listened to her guiding bell ; its cheerful tinkle proclaiming the route clear along narrow dizzy ledge, or through deep defile. And now he will hear its music no more.

But the ties must be severed, the parting take place. Which it does, amidst phrases and ejaculations of leave-taking, tender as though the left ones were human beings instead of dumb brutes. "*Caballo—caballito querido !*" "*Mula-mulita mia !*" "*Pobre-pobrecita ! Dios te guarda!*" And mingled with these are exclamations of a less gentle kind — anathemas hurled at the red-skins coming on to take possession of their pets.

At this last Pedro Vicente is among the loudest. As yet he has had only half-payment for his late discovered mine, the remaining moiety dependent on the working it. And now the crash—all the mining apparatus to be destroyed—perhaps the purchasing firm made bankrupt, if even life be left them. Thinking of all this, and what he has already suffered at the hands of "*Los Indios*," no wonder at his cursing them. He, however, is not one of those taking affectionate and sentimental farewell of their animals. His horse is a late purchase, and though of fine appearance, has proved aught but a bargain. For there are "copers" in Arispe as elsewhere, and the *gambusino* has been their victim. Hence he parts with the disappointing steed neither regretfully nor reluctantly. But not with the saddle and bridle; these, of elaborate adornment having cost him far more than the horse. So shouldering them, he too re-ascends, last of all save one.

That one is Henry Tresillian; and very different is the parting between him and the animal of his belonging. The English youth almost sheds tears as he stands by his horse's head, patting his neck and stroking his muzzle, the last time he may ever lay hand on either. Nay, surely, too surely, the last. And the noble creature seems to know it too, responding to the caress by a low mournful whimpering.

"Ah! my beautiful Crusader! to think I must leave you behind! And to be ridden by a red-skin—a cruel savage who will take no care of you. Oh! it is hard—hard!"

Crusader appears to comprehend what is said, for his answer is something like a moan. It may be that he interprets the melancholy expression on his master's face—that master who has been so kind to him.

"A last farewell, brave fellow! Be it a kiss,"

says the youth, bringing his lips in contact with those of the horse. Then pulling off the head-stall, with its attached trail-rope, and letting them drop to the ground, he again speaks the sad word "farewell," and, turning back on his beloved steed, walks hurriedly and determinedly away, as though fearing resolution might fail him.

Soon he commences climbing up the gorge; all the others who have gone before now nearly out of it. But ere he has ascended ten steps, he hears that behind which causes him to stop and look back. Not in alarm: he knows it to be the neigh of his own horse, accompanied by the stroke of his hoofs in quick repetition—Crusader coming on in a gallop for the gorge. In another instant he is by its bottom, on hind legs, rearing up against the rocky steep, as if determined to scale it.

In vain: after an effort he drops back on all fours. But to rear up and try again and again, all the while giving utterance to wild, agonized neighs—very screams

To Henry Tresillian the sight is saddening, the sound torture, stirring his heart to its deepest depths. To escape the seeing—though he cannot so soon the hearing—he once more turns his back upon the horse, and hastens on upward. But when half-way to the head, he cannot resist taking another downward look. Which shows him Crusader yet by the bottom of the gorge, but now standing still on all fours, as if resigned to the inevitable. Not silent, however; instead, at short intervals, giving utterance to that neigh of melancholy cadence, alike proclaiming discomfiture and despair.

CHAPTER IX.

"IT'S THE RATTLESNAKE."

On again reaching the summit Henry Tresillian finds his father there with Don Estevan
and most of the men. These last, under the
direction of the *ci-devant* soldier, are collecting
large stones, and laying them all round the head
of the gorge.

One might fancy them building a breastwork,
but nothing of that kind is their intention, none
such being needed. As Vicente had said, it is
a fortress of nature's construction, stronger than
any ever built by the hand of man, and would
defy breaching by all the artillery in the world.
Ammunition is what the stones are being collected for, to be rolled down the slope in case
the enemy should attempt scaling it. Most of
them have to be brought up out of the gorge

itself, as but few lie loose on the summit. A work that, with so many and willing hands, takes up but short time, and soon a ridge appears in horseshoe shape around the spot where the path leads out upon the level.

Others of the men have gone on to the glade by the spring, where the women and children are now assembled, the effects brought up from below lying scattered about them. Some, still in affright, are moving excitedly to and fro; others, with greater courage and calmness, have taken seats on the boxes and bundles.

The señora and her daughter, with the family servants, form a group apart, the eyes of Gertrude scanning with anxious interrogative glance each new party as it appears on the edge of the opening. She has been told that Henrique is still upon the plain, and fears he may linger there too long.

As yet no move has been made to set up the tents, or otherwise establish camp. There are some who cling to the hope that after all it may not be necessary. The Indians have

not yet shown themselves at the southern end,
and nothing is known of their character save
by conjecture. As that is based on but a distant view of them, it is little reliable; and the
guide is directed by Don Estevan to hasten
north again, and see what can be seen further.

This time he takes the telescope with him,
and signals are arranged before starting. Gun
signals, of course : a single shot to say the
Indians are still advancing towards the Cerro;
two, that they are near ; a third, denoting their
character made out ; while a fourth will proclaim them *bravos*, and of some hostile tribe.

By this it might appear as if the *gambusino*
bore upon his person a very battery of small
arms; while in reality he has only his rifle, with
a pair of single-barrelled pistols of ancient
fashion and doubtful fire. But, as before, he
is to be accompanied by Henry Tresillian,
whose double gun will make good any defi-
ciency in the signal shots—should all four be
needed.

This settled, off the two go again on their old

track, first passing through the glade by the *ojo de agua.* There the English youth tarries a moment — only a brief one — to exchange a word with the señora, and a tender glance with Gertrude, whose eyes follow him no longer in fear, but now all admiration. She has been told of the strange parting between him and his favourite steed—her favourite as well—and the fearlessness he displayed, staying down upon the plain after all the others had left it.

"Such courage!" she mentally exclaims, as she sees him dash on after the guide. "*Dios mio!* he dare do anything."

Proceeding at a run, in less than fifteen minutes' time the videttes arrive at their former place of observation on the projecting point of the cliff; and without delay Vicente lengthens out the telescope, raising it to his eye. To see, at first view, what justifies their sounding the first and second signals: the savages still coming on for the Cerro, and now near!

"Fire off both your barrels!" he directs on the instant; and, without lowering the glass,

"Allow a little time between, that our people mayn't mistake it for a single shot."

The English youth, elevating the muzzle of his gun, presses the front trigger, and then, after an interval, the back one, and the shots in succession go reverberating along the cliff in echo upon echo.

Scarce have these died away when the Mexican again speaks, this time not only to say the other two signals are to be given, but with words and in tone telling of even more. "*Carramba!*" he cries out, "just as I expected, and worse! Apaches, and the cruellest, most hostile of all, Coyoreros! Quick, *muchacho!*" he continues, still keeping the telescope to his eye, "pull the pistols out of my belt and fire off both."

Again two loud cracks, with a few seconds of time between, resound along the cliff, while the dusky horsemen, now near enough for their individual forms to be distinguishable by the naked eye, are seen to have come to a halt, seated on their horses and gazing upward. But through the glass Vicente sees more, which still further excites him.

"*Por todos demonios esta El Cascabel!*" (By all the devils it's the Rattlesnake!)

"El Cascabel!" echoes the English youth, less puzzled by the odd name than surprised at the manner of him who has pronounced it. "Who is he, Don Pedro?"

"Ah, señorito! you'll find that out too soon —all of us, I fear, to our cost. Yes!" he goes on talking, with the telescope still upheld, "'t is El Cascabel, I can make out the death's head on his breast, original pattern of that on my own. He and his made the copy, the brutes burning it into my flesh in sheer wanton mockery. *Malraya!* we're in for it now; a siege till the crack of doom, or till all of us are starved dead. No hope of escaping it."

"But if we surrender, might they not be merciful?"

"Merciful! surrender to the Rattlesnake! That would be as putting ourselves in the

power of the reptile he takes his name from.
You forget Gil Perez and his massacre."

"No, indeed. But was it Coyoteros he
massacred?"

"Coyoteros; and of this very band. El
Cascabel's not like to have forgotten that;
and will now make us innocent people pay for
it. *Ay de mi!*"

With this final exclamation, uttered in a tone
of deep despondence, the Mexican relapses into
silence. But only for a few seconds longer, to
look through the telescope. He has seen
enough to know all which can be known, and
too truly conjectures what is likely to ensue.

The party of Indians, led by El Cascabel, is
again moving onward, and a sweep of the glass
around to the north-west shows the other party
making to turn the mountain on its western
side. The *gambusino* can count them now; sees
that they number over two hundred, enough
to put all hope of a successful encounter with
them out of the question. As for retreat, it is
too late for that. Surrounded are the luckless

miners, or soon will be; besieged on the summit of a mountain as within the walls of a fortress, and as far removed from any chance of succour as castaways on a desert isle in mid-ocean.

CHAPTER X.

THE "stone artillery" has been got together; a huge pile of it, forming at the same time protecting parapet and battery of guns; the men have desisted from their work, and having nothing more to do, at least for a time, stand listening for the signals. They know that such have been arranged, without having been told their exact bearing.

But they are soon to learn it; almost instantly after hearing a shot, and then quick succeeding it another, as the discharges from a double-barrelled gun.

"The Indians coming on, and near!" says Don Estevan, interpreting to those around. "We may look to see them soon yonder."

He nods towards the abandoned camp, a

portion of which is visible from the head of the gorge.

This causes a turning of all eyes in its direction, and on the *llano* beyond. But scarce have they commenced scanning it when two other shots, less loud but with a like interval between, reach their ears, proceeding from the same quarter.

" The pistols—signals three and four ! " mechanically pronounces the ex-officer of dragoons, his sallow features showing further clouded. " There's no more to listen for now," he adds. " Don Pedro was right. Apaches they must be, and on a marauding expedition — likely for the towns of the Horcasitas, and, unluckily, we in their way. Ah, *amigos !* it's an ill look-out for us ; could not well be worse."

But worse it is, as they are yet to learn. And soon do learn from the lips of the *gambusino*, who, returning in breathless haste, cries out ere he is up to them,

" *Los Coyoteros !* The band of El Cascabel ! "

Words of terrible portent, needing no ex-

planation, for they recall to the minds of all
present that sanguinary incident already alluded
to. The dastardly deed of Captain Perez and
his ruffianly soldiery is likely to be retaliated on
men, not only themselves guiltless, but every
one of whom has condemned it! For how can
they expect mercy from the friends and relatives
of his murdered victims? How hope for any
distinction or exception in their favour? They
cannot, and do not, knowing that ever since that
inhuman massacre the Apaches have treated
every pale-face as a foe, the Coyoteros killing
all prisoners that fall into their hands, after
torturing them.

" You think it 's the band of Cascabel ? "

It is Don Estevan who questions in rejoinder
to the *gambusino's* brief but expressive report.

" Think! I 'm sure of it, your worship.
Through this good glass of yours I recognized
that savage himself, knowing him too well. It
enabled me to make out his *totem*, the pretty
device on his breast, of which this on mine 's
but a poor copy. *Mira !* "

While speaking, he unbuttons his shirt-front and draws the plaits apart, as a screen from some precious picture, exposing to the view of all what he had already shown to Henry Tresillian. As most of them remember having heard of the sepulchral symbol borne by the Coyotero chief, with that other more appropriate to his name, they now know the sort of enemy that is approaching, and what they have to expect. No more among them is there hope of either friendship or mercy. On one side, the stronger, it will be attack hostile and vengeful; on the other, and weaker—theirs, alas!—it must be resistance and defence even unto death.

Though fully convinced of this, the miners remain calm, with that confidence due to danger seeming still distant. They know they are safe for the time, unassailable, the *gambusino* having given them assurance of it. But they now see it for themselves, and any apprehensions they have are less for the present than the future. Sure are they that a siege is before them, how long they cannot guess, nor in which way it will terminate. And there may be chances of relief or escape they have not thought of. Hope is hard to kill, and the least hopeful of them has not yet yielded to despair. Time enough for that when starvation stares them in the face, for hunger—famine—is the foe they have most to fear.

But they think not of things so far ahead. They must first see the enemy of which their guide has given such awe-inspiring account; and, with glances sent abroad and over that portion of the plain visible to them, they await his appearance on it.

Nearly another hour elapses without any enemy seen. The horses and mules have got over their late excitement, and are again tranquilly depasturing, some having waded into the lake to cool their hoofs, still hot after their long *jornada*. But none wander away from the proximity of the camp; the only animals out on the plain being prong-horn antelopes, a herd of which, on their way to the water too, has been deterred approaching it by the presence of huge monsters unknown to them—the wagons. But these have not hindered the approach of the black-winged birds; instead, attracted them, and a large flock is now around the abandoned camp, some wheeling above, others at rest on the ground or perched upon the rock-boulders which bestrew it. A crowd, collected on the spot where the ox had been butchered for breakfast, contest possession of its offal.

All of a sudden, and simultaneously, a movement is perceptible among the animals, birds as quadrupeds, the wild as the tame. The pronghorns with a snort raise their heads aloft as if they saw or scented some new danger, then lope off at lightning speed. The vultures take wing, but only rise a little way into the air, to soar round in circles; while the horses, mules, and horned cattle, as if seized by a frenzy of madness, rush excitedly about, wildly neighing and bellowing, at each instant threatening to break away in stampede.

"They smell redskin," knowingly observes the *gambusino*, who is among the rest watching their movements. "Yes; and we'll soon see the ugly thing itself. *Chingara !* yonder it is."

He has no need to point out either the thing or the place. The eyes of all are now on it; the head of a dusky cohort just appearing round the eastern projection of the Cerro, becoming elongated as file after file unfolds itself. They are still afar off—at least a league—nor is their line of march directed towards the mountain, but westward, as though they intended turning it.

No such manœuvre is meant, however, as the miners, forewarned by their guide, are already aware. His words are made good by their seeing soon after another dark line developing itself on the *llano*, at a like distance off, but coming from the opposite direction.

"The party that went west about," says the *gambusino*, half in soliloquy; "cunning in them to make a complete surround of us. I suppose they thought we were but horsemen, and might

THE ENFILADING LINE.—p. 102

get away from them. If they'd seen our wagons, it would have saved them some trouble. Well, they see everything now."

No one makes rejoinder, all intently gazing at the two marching bands, now with eyes on one, then quickly transferred to the other. The portion of the plain visible is sextant-shaped— the view on either side cut off by the flanking ridges of the ravine—and from each side the string of savage horsemen is continuously lengthening out. Not rapidly, but in slow leisurely crawl, as if confident they had already secured the enfiladement of the camp. With a thicker concentration near the head of each, and a metallic sparkle all along their line—the sheen of their armour under the rays of the meridian sun—they appear as two huge serpents of ante-diluvian age, deliberately drawing towards one another either for friendship or combat.

In due time their front files come together, near the central part of the sextant; though the rear ones are still invisible;—how many of these no one knows, save approximately.

Enough, however, are already in sight to make a formidable array, and put all thought of conflict with them out of the question. The miners but congratulate themselves on their fortune in finding that secure place of retreat, which will enable them to shun it. Grateful are they to their guide for making it known—and they have reason. If within their late camp instead of where they now are, the hours of their life would be numbered—perhaps to count only minutes. At the best they could but save bare life for a time, but nothing to comfort or sustain it.

All this they have come to comprehend thoroughly as they continue to watch the movements of the Coyoteros, and see the cordon these have drawn around them. But for some minutes there is no movement at all, the bands after uniting having come to a halt, the files making quarter-wheel, so as to face the Cerro —all done as by trained cavalry on a parade-ground! And for a while they stay halted, the change of front giving their alignment a thinner look. But at the central point is a thicker clump, without military formation, on which Don Estevan directs his telescope. To see half a dozen of the mounted savages face to face with one another, earnestly, excitedly gesticulating. After a look through it, he tenders the glass to the *gambusino*, who may better understand what they are about.

"El Cascabel and his sub-chiefs in consultation," pronounces the latter, soon as sighting them. "It's plain they're puzzled by seeing wagons where never were such before. Like as not they think we're *soldados*, and that makes them cautious. But they'll soon know different. *Por Dios!* they know it now. They're coming on!"

CHAPTER XI.

THE *gambusino* has guessed everything aright, if words spoken in the confidence of knowledge can be called guesses. True they prove, to the spirit as the letter; for it is just that unaccustomed spectacle of wheeled vehicles with their white canvas covers that caused the Indians to keep their deploying line so far aloof, and bring it to a halt for deliberation. Notwithstanding their being masters of all that desert country, lords of the *llanos*, they themselves do not always traverse it without difficulties to encounter and dangers to dread. The wagons proclaim the camp occupied by white men; and knowing these to be ordinary travellers, miners on the move, or *commerciantes* on a trading expedition to the frontier towns,

106

the Coyoteros would little regard them—certainly not enough to have made that long *détour* with so much delay in approaching them. But it may be a *military* encampment; and if so, will need to be dealt with differently—hence their unwonted caution.

Soon as the two bands became conjoined, El Cascabel had summoned his sub-chiefs around him, to take their opinions upon this point. For among Indians the head chief is not armed with despotic authority, but must submit his intended course of action to the approval of his following, even when on the *maraud.* And as the *gambusino* rightly conjectured, this it was which occupied them at that temporary halt.

A question without difficulty, and soon decided. In the negative as regarded the camp being occupied by soldiers. Were it so, men in uniform would be observable around it; whereas none such are seen. Nor human form of any kind; only animals—horses, and mules, with horned cattle commingled—all careering madly about as if masterless, or escaped from their masters' control.

This might seem an odd circumstance, yet it does not to the savages. From experience they know that all animals belonging to the pale-faces become affrighted at their own proximity—often to break from their fastenings, however secure. Such a scare is likely what they see now.

All the more does it assure them they will not have to deal with *soldados.* These would have their horses under better discipline, would indeed by this time be on their backs, at least some of them.

Satisfied of its being a camp of civilians, at a signal sent along their line the red horsemen make a move forward, their files becoming thicker as the cordon contracts into nearer and narrower curve. Still they advance slowly, not through fear or want of confidence, but because they feel sure their enfiladement is complete, and their victims enclosed. But another idea rules their cautious approach. A splendid prize is before them in that large *ca Callada*, and to ride hurriedly in might lead to the loose animals breaking through their ranks, and scattering off over the plain, with after difficulty of capturing them. For just then they might have enough to do with their owners. Besides, there can be no surprise. The occupants of the camp, whoever they be, must have seen them long since, and are watching them now, though not one of themselves can be seen. Nothing so strange in this; they are inside the wagon enclosure, screened by the ridge of *alparejas* that form a sort of breastwork around it. And the ruck of frightened animals rushing to and fro between further prevents view of them. The more reason for deliberate approach, this attitude of the white men telling of an intention to stand upon the defence.

Becoming convinced of this, the Indians give up thought of immediate attack. They will wait for the night's darkness to give them a better opportunity; and when at such a distance as they deem beyond longest gun range, they again come to a halt.

They would dismount, holding their horses in readiness; and some are already on the ground. But before all alight, a word is sent along their circular line, ordering them up' again. Something has transpired to give cause for a change of purpose.

Soon they know what, seeing that the camp animals have retreated back beyond the wagons up into an embayment of the cliff, where they stand in a clump, cowering and still showing scare, but at rest. It is not that, however, which has made the Coyoteros re-mount, but because their view of the camp now being clear they still cannot see human beings in or around it. With eyes bent in keenest quest between the corraled wagons, through the spokes of their wheels, all along the periphery of pack-saddles, nothing in the shape of human form or face can they make out. Yet the sun is in their favour, and if such was there they could not fail seeing it. Puzzled are the savages

now, and for the first time—since it is the first
time for them to have such an experience.
For the moment it even mystifies them, and
thoughts of the supernatural come creeping into
their minds. They know Nauchampa-tepetl to
be a place of weird repute, so figuring in many
a record and legend of their race. And now
to see a camp there, a camp of the pale-faces,
with every appointment appertaining, wheeled
vehicles drawn up in *corral* with a grand tent
inside—for the marquee, still standing, is conspicuous through a break between the wagons
—with all the animals that should be there, and
yet no man, no one seeming to own or control
them, that is certainly strange, to the point of
astonishment—even awe !

And for a time it so affects the savage
warriors, their chief not excepted. But only
for a time. Notwithstanding his ghostly coat-
of-arms, El Cascabel is but little the slave of
superstition ; and, after a moment's reflection,
feels satisfied there are pale-faces in the camp,
though invisible to the view of him and his.

In that, as the reader knows, he is wrong; but right in the way he takes to test it.

It may seem the veriest *grotesquerie* here to introduce that venerated weapon, known as the "Queen Anne musket," yet the truthfulness of this record requires its introduction.

For strange as it may appear, this historical piece, with all its imperfections, has found its way to every corner of the world; even into the hands of the Apache Indians. How they became possessed of it needs but a word of explanation, which is, that they had it—took it—from their hereditary enemies, the Mexicans—from the *infanterio* of that nation, armed with the old condemned "Queen Anne's" of London Tower celebrity.

Leaving this necessary digression, and returning to the Coyoteros—more especially to their chief, we hear him call out to those of his followers who carry the ancient firelock, giving them orders to advance some paces and send shots into the white man's camp.

Dismounting, they do so, aiming at the

THE COYOTEROS FLYING INTO THE CORRAL.—p. 11.

UNIV
CALIF.

wagons and tent inside, so correctly that their big bullets, an ounce in weight, are seen to hit the mark. But without effect following, any more than if their shots were meant for the *façade* of cliff beyond, whose rocks echo back the reports of the antiquated pieces, as if in hilarious mockery.

CHAPTER XII.

THE CHASE OF CRUSADER.

By El Cascabel's orders, repeatedly are the big muskets re-loaded and fired into the *corral*, till every wagon has had a bullet through it, and the tent is pierced in several places. But all with the same effect, the shots eliciting no other response than their own echoes. Now the Indians know for sure that the camp is unoccupied; and, but for their foreknowledge of the topography of the place, would be mystified indeed. But most of them have themselves been on the summit of Nauchampa-tapetl, and their eyes turn interrogatively towards it. Thither the white men must have retreated, leaving everything below.

They see nothing, however; not as much as a face. For Don Estevan has directed those by the head of the gorge to keep well under cover, in hopes of tempting the savages to an ascent in the face of his formidable battery.

But the Coyotero chief is too astute for that, knowing, moreover, that there is no chance for the despised enemy to escape him. Wrathful he is withal, at having been in a way outwitted, angry at himself for having made the surround so slowly. It will cost him a siege, he knows not how long, interfering with the expedition to the Horcasitas, perhaps to its abandonment. But there is some compensation in the plunder so unexpectedly come upon, and from what he sees it should be an ample one. Six large wagons with a grand *tienda—litera* also—visible, to say nothing of the numerous animals, a travelling party so well appointed should also have commodities in correspondence, promising a rich prize.

The camp is good as captured already; but instead of hastening on to take possession, he proceeds slowly and systematically as ever; for nothing can be gained by speed now, and something may be lost—the loose animals. They are still crowded up in the embayment between the cliffs, but with heads aloft and ears apeak, neighing, snorting, and restless, as if about to make a break.

"Leave aside arms, all—guns, and spears!" commands the chief. "Get ready the *riatas!*"

All together drop down from their horses, those who carry spears sticking them upright in the ground, those with firelocks laying them along it. Any *impedimenta* of baggage and accoutrements are also pulled off and flung beside. Then they vault back upon their animals, each with but his trail-rope carried in coil over the left arm, to be used as a *lazo.*

Thus disencumbered and equipped, they at length advance, not for the camp, but the *caballada;* but ere they can close up the mouth of the cove the white men's animals become more affrighted than ever, and make the burst they had been threatening—horses, mules, and oxen all together. With a noise of thunder, the ground echoes the tread of their hundreds of

hooves, as in frenzied madness they rush out
for the open plain. Little chance would there
be of their reaching it but that the Indian
horses catch the stampede, too, many of them
becoming unmanageable. The enfilading line
is broken, and through its riven ranks the camp
animals sweep as a hurricane. One is in the
lead—a large horse, coal black, on whom many
an Indian had set eye, with *lazo* ready for his
capture. Crusader it is, his neigh heard above
all others, as, with head on high, mane tossed,
and tail streaming afar, he dashes at the severed
line ; again uttered, as it were exultingly, when,
having cleared it, he sees no enemy before him.
Half a dozen nooses are flung at and after him,
all ill-directed ; all fall short, and slide from his
glistening flanks, while as many disappointed
cries follow him in chorus.

All is scamper and confusion now ; the
surround has failed, the stampede taken place,
and the stampeded animals, such as succeeded
in getting off—for not all went clear—can only
be captured after a chase. But the Indian

horses quickly get over their scare, and are laid on the pursuit till a stream of them stretches out on the *llano*. Fresher and in better condition than the camp animals, these are soon overtaken and noosed, now one, now another, till at length only a single horse is seen beyond the pursuing line.

Followed still, but so far beyond it, at each bound widening the distance, that a pair of eyes watching the chase, at first apprehensively, now sparkle with delight. For they are the eyes of his own master, Henry Tresillian, standing on the *mesa's* summit behind a screening tree.

Half a score of the savages still continue the pursuit, among them their chief himself. For he would give much to be the owner of that matchless steed, and now strains his own to the utmost. All in vain. Crusader forges farther and farther away, till he is but a speck upon the plain. Then the baffled pursuers, one after another, give up discouraged, at length El Cascabel also coming to a stop, and turning to ride back with an air of angry disappointment.

The English youth, yielding to a thrill of proud exultation, waves his cap in the air, giving utterance to a triumphant "Hurrah!"

"I'm so glad he's got away from them," he says, to Vicente, by his side; "wherever he may go or whatever become of him. My noble Crusader! But wasn't it clever? Wasn't it grand?"

"Wonderful!" responds the *gambusino*, alike moved to admiration. "I never saw horse behave so in all my born life. *Santissima!* he must be a witch, if not the *demonio* himself."

*   *   *   *   *

The Indians, leading back the captured animals, and recovering their arms, no longer delay entering the camp. Which, to their chagrin, they find not only abandoned, but wellnigh despoiled, as if other plunderers had been there before them! That much has been carried off, and of course of the most valuable kind, is evinced by boxes broken open, bales unroped and the contents extracted, with here and there empty spaces in the wagons, where

evidently something had been stored. There
is little left for them save the refuse, or effects
of a nature to be of no use to them. What care
they for mining tools and machinery?

More than ever are they angry and regretful
of their ill-judged delay; but vow deadlier vengeance, when the time comes for it.

Still that may not be soon. The very fashion
of retreat shows it to have been made with
deliberation, and that the white men intend
standing a siege, with the hopes and the where-
withal to hold out ever so long. And they, the
Indians, knowing the danger of breasting that
steep in the face of resolute defenders, have no
thought of attempting it. But the goods that
have been carried up must remain there, and
sooner or later fall into their hands.

So consoling themselves, the new occupants
of the camp settle down to the siege, after
having secured their animals—both their own
and those they have just come into possession
of. All are put out to grass, "hoppled" or
tethered on trail-ropes. Then the fires, found

smouldering, are replenished with fresh fuel, and blaze up brightly as ever, with spits and roasting joints all round them.

This day the Coyoteros dine on beef, instead of their customary diet of *mezcal* and baked horseflesh. And a plenteous repast they make. Not for a long time have they had such an opportunity of gormandizing. In their desert land of Apacheria provisions are scarce—often to starvation-point; and they now feast gluttonously, as if to make up for many a fast.

Nor are they without drinkables, though none brought they along with them. In a corner of one of the wagons is a cask—which on being tapped is found to be filled with *chingarita*—a fiery spirit distilled from the very plant, chief staple of their food—the *mezcal.* The Coyoteros know it well, and though they do not themselves distil, they drink it, and are so fond of it as to wonder why the cask is there, and not also carried up the mountain!

Drawn out, and rolled to the middle of the *corral,* they dance in delight around it, re-

peatedly quaffing from their calabash cups, with
such an accompaniment of noises that the camp,
lately occupied by men and women, might seem
to have come into the possession of devils.

And so on till night. Then demon-like indeed are the forms seen flitting around its fires,
and as much the faces, lit up by the red glare
from blazing fagots of *mezquite* and *piñon*—both
resinous trees. Still more the discordant sounds,
a chorus of cries and ejaculations, in mad wild
yelling, as of Bedlam broke loose.

CHAPTER XIII.

A RETRIBUTIVE SHOT.

IT is midnight, and darkness over mountain and plain; pitch darkness, although there is a moon in the sky. But she is not visible, obscured by a bank of thick cumulous clouds, that have rolled up from the Californian Gulf—portent of an approaching rain-storm.

The savages have gone to rest; or, at all events, brought their noisy revelry to an end, and silence reigns everywhere around, save now and then a snort from a miner's horse, or mule, with a stamp of hoof, uneasy in their new companionship; the half howl, half bark of prowling coyote, and the wailing of Chuck-will's-widow—the nightjar of Sonora—hawking for insects high over the lake. But no sound of human voice is heard, nor through the inky blackness can be seen form of man.

Yet not all are asleep, either above or below. On the plain is a line of sentries, set at distances apart on the outer edge of the triangular space where the path goes up ; and inside this, by the bottom of the gorge itself, two other men, though not on sentinel duty.

All Indians, of course ; one of the pair by themselves being El Cascabel, the other a subchief, his second in command. They are there on reconnoitring purposes, to discover whether it be possible for the besiegers to make the ascent on a dark night unseen, and so take the besieged by surprise.

Since settling down in camp the Rattlesnake has reflected, and a thought is now in his mind making him uneasy. Not regret for having to forego his raid on the settlements of the Horcasitas. Unlikely that the siege would take up any more time, and the booty alone should be ample compensation. For he has made study of the abandoned camp, found every indication of wealth, and feels sure it late held rich treasures. They would reward him for the time lost in beleaguering. And as to the revenge, a whole company of miners—nigh a hundred at least—with their wives and daughters, grand señoras among them too—death to the men, and captivity to the women—that should satisfy the keenest vengeance.

And perhaps it would his, were he sure of accomplishing it. He was before the sun went down, but is not now. For, since, he has thought of that which had not then occurred to him or to any of his following. Might not the miners have sent off a courier back to their own country, with a demand for help? If so, it would surely come; in strength sufficient, and soon enough to raise the siege. For the head men of the besieging force now know it will be a prolonged one. The fragments of provisions found in the wagons tell of a good store taken out of them and up. Game is there in abundance to supplement it, and water never-failing —a fortress in every way supplied. Not so strange, then, the Coyotero chief being nervous at the thought of a courier having been dispatched. For one might, without having been seen by him or his. A long distance it was from where they themselves must have been first sighted by those on the mountain.

But for the obscurity, there are those on it who would see himself and his second now. By the head of the gorge above a party of miners keep guard. They have just come on duty, the relief after a spell of sleep. For Don Estevan, by old experience, knowing there was no danger of Indian attack in the earlier hours, had entrusted the guard-keeping of these to the more common men. Between midnight and morning is the time to "'ware red-skin," and the guard of this period, now commenced, has been confided to a picked party, two of those composing it being Pedro Vicente and his *fidus achates*, Henry Tresillian.

Guard it can scarce be called, being only a small vidette-picket. For there is little fear—scarce a thought—that the Indians will attempt the ascent, at least not so soon, or without gravely reflecting upon it.

"Perhaps never at all," says the *gambusino*, in confabulation with his fellow-watchers. "And why should they? They must be well aware of the chances against them. Besides, having got us as fish in a net, they're not likely to leap into the water themselves, where they know there are *tiburones* (sharks)."

Vicente has had a spell at pearl-diving in the Gulf, hence his simile drawn from the sea.

"Ay, *tintoreros*—these," he adds, specifying the most dreaded of the squaline tribe, with hand caressingly rested on one of the large stones alongside which he is lying. "I only wish they *would* try it, the Rattlesnake leading. 'T would give me just the opportunity I want to pay that artist off for the bit of bad engraving he did on my breast—by hurling one of these beauties at his head. *Malraya!* I may never have the chance to settle that score—not likely now."

The final words, uttered in a tone of angry

disappointed vengeance, are followed by an interval of silence. For the new videttes, having just entered on their duty, deem it wise, before aught else, to make themselves acquainted with how matters are below. They are all in recumbent attitude, *ventre à terre*, behind the parapet of loose stones. For having witnessed that long-range practice with the "Queen Annes," it occurs to them that a big bullet may at any moment come whizzing up the gorge, and just as well be out of its way. So elevating but their eyes over, they look cautiously down. To see nothing—not even the plain, nor yet the lake; to hear nothing which proceeds from human kind; but they know the savages are on the alert, with sentries aligned below, and for a time continue to listen.

At length, satisfied there is nothing which calls for their vigilance being kept on the strain, Vicente draws out his *cajoncito* of corn-husk *cigarittos*, lights one, and sets to smoking. His comrades of the watch do likewise; and the English youth, long since initiated into the ways of the country, smokes too, only his weed is a Havannah.

Not many minutes are they thus occupied when the *gambusino*, chancing to turn his eyes south-westward, sees what makes him spit the *cigarillo* from his mouth, and gaze intently. The object is up in the sky; a slight rift just opened in the bank of cloud, edged yellowish-white. The moon must be near it—*is* near it, and now in it! for while they are still regarding the blue spot, she shoots suddenly out from the black, as arrow from bow.

Instantly night's darkness is turned into light as of day; every object on the *llano*, even the smallest, made visible for miles upon miles, up to the horizon's verge. But their eyes go not so far, least of all those of Pedro Vicente, who at the first flash from the unveiled moon catches sight of that which arrests his straying glances, fixing them fast. Not the line of sentries, though he sees them too; but a pair of figures inside and closer, up nigh the point where the path steps upon the plain. One of them,

recognized, rivets his gaze by a token of iden-
tification unmistakable — a death's head in
white chalk, which, with the moon full upon
it, gleams conspicuous against a background
of bronze.

" *Carria!* El Cascabel!" he mechanically
mutters, in tone of exultation; and without
saying another word, or waiting another second,
brings his rifle to shoulder, the stock to his
cheek, with muzzle deep depressed.

A blaze—a crack—and the bullet is sped.
A cry of agony from below—another of anger
in voice different — proclaims its course true,
and that the mark aimed at has been hit.

He who fired the shot knows that, by sight
as well as sound. For he sees—all see—a man
reeling, staggering, about to fall, and another
with arms outstretched, as if partly in surprise,
partly with intent to support him.

Only for an instant is the spectacle under
their eyes. For suddenly as she showed herself, the moon disappears with a plunge into
the opaque clouds, leaving all dark as before.

CHAPTER XIV.

THE "DEATH FANDANGO."

"You think you've killed him?"

It is Don Estevan who interrogates, startled out of his slumber by the report of the *gambusino's* gun, which has brought him in hurried haste to the post of guard.

"Pretty sure of it, your worship," is the rejoinder, in calm confidence.

"We all saw him staggering—he must have gone down," says another of the videttes, confirmingly.

"If I haven't settled his hash," pursues Vicente, "then a man may get a bullet through midribs, and live afterwards—a thing not likely. Or I'm much mistaken, mine went straight centreways into the white—that sweet thing

I've such reason to remember—unluckily for him painted too conspicuously."

"It must have been El Cascabel, if you saw that."

"He it was, or I shouldn't have been so quick on the trigger. Indeed, I wasn't so confident about the carry of my piece. 'T was a long shot."

"The bullet may have hit without killing him—spent, and only stunned him?"

"If your worship feels inclined for a bet, I'll lay big odds that ere this the Rattlesnake has kicked his last kick, or, to put it more appropriately, wriggled his last wriggle."

The auditory gathered around the *gambusino* would laugh at his quaint words, but ere they give way to the inclination it is checked by other words quick following in exclamatory tones,

"Bet's off, your worship—too late! I'm not the man to dishonour myself by wagering on a certainty. *Oigate!* you hear that?"

Don Estevan does hear, as the others, sounds

ascending from below—human voices, in that melancholy cadence which tells of lamentation for the dead. They come from the direction of the camp, in a wild crooning wail, now and then a stave, as if coyotes were taking part in the lugubrious chorus. At intervals, also, there are other notes, differently intoned; loud angry ejaculations, the Apache war-cry, proclaiming vengeance only to be satisfied with blood for blood.

For nearly an hour the infernal *fracas* is kept up, the volume of voice continuous, and redoubled by reverberation along the cliffs. Then it is abruptly brought to a close, succeeded by a silence mysterious and ominous in itself. Can it be that in their insane anger the savages have resolved upon the ascent, *coûte-qui-coûte?* The darkness, dense as ever, would favour, and might tempt them.

There is enough probability in it to make the videttes more vigilant, and their numbers are now greater. After an event of such serious consequence, most of the people—women and

children excepted—are up and active, moving
backwards and forwards between their place of
bivouac by the spring and the ravine's head,
all careful not to approach this point too near.
The big muskets admonish them; though as
yet no shot from one, nor from any other sort
of piece, has been fired by the savages. If
they mean assault, it will be by stealth, and in
silence.

Hushed, and listening with all ears, the
watchers hear nothing; at least, no sound of
a suspicious nature. But Indians can creep, or
climb, noiselessly as cats—the Coyoteros especially—in this respect equalling the animal
from which they have their name. And they
may be worming their way up for all, snake-like
among the stems of the *mesquites* and cactus
plants.

"Speaking for myself," says the *gambusino*,
after a time, "I haven't much fear of them
trying that trick. But if you think it worth
while, *camarados*, to give them a hint—and
perhaps it may be as well—we can spare a few

of these pebbles." He points to the collected stones. "Half a dozen or so will do it."

His *camarados* comprehend his meaning; and as Don Estevan has returned to his tent leaving him in command of the picket, they signify their approval of his design, all desiring it.

On the instant after, a rock pushed over the edge goes crashing down, breaking off branches, loosening other stones in its way, all in loud rumbling borne together to the level below. But they elicit no response, save the echo of their own noise, no shriek or cry, as if man were caught and bruised by them.

After a time another is launched, with like result, then another and another at measured intervals—for they must husband their ammunition—the watchers all the while without fear that man, red or white, will face such an avalanche, dangerous as any that ever swept down the slope of Alps.

At the earliest dawn they desist as soon as they can trust to their eyes. And now, scanning the plain below, they see at the bottom of the gorge only the rocks they had rolled down, with the other *débris.* Farther out they perceive the line of dusky sentinels, just as they expected it to be; but no other human form, living or dead. The Coyotero chief is dead for all that—carried to the camp of the pale-faces, inside the great tent, where he now lies face upward; the pale, crepusculous light stealing in to show that hideous device on his breast, symbol of death itself, no longer a disc of white, but flaked and mottled red, with a darker spot of ragged edging in the centre where it was pierced by the *gambusino's* bullet.

*   *   *   *   *

Just as the sun begins to show above the horizon's edge, again go up the crooning cries, but now in more measured strain. For the savages are collected in the *corral,* a choice party of them under direction of their medicine man ranged about the marquee, not standing still, but circling round and round it in a slow, saltatory step — in short, dancing the "death-dance."

It is accompanied by chants and incantations, in the voice of the medicine chief himself, pitched louder than the rest, with a pause at intervals, to speak eulogies of the deceased, praise of his valour and virtues, ending in a passionate appeal to his followers to avenge his death. They need not the stimulus of such exhortation. In the eyes of all vengeance is already glowing, burning, and but flashes a little angrier as they respond in a vociferous and united yell.

They upon the *mesa* are not witnesses to this odd ceremony, only a portion of the camp being within their view. But ere long they have another under their eyes — a spectacle equally exciting, and of like grave portent to themselves.

It takes place out on the open plain by the lake's edge, upon a portion of the grass ground, all visible from the ravine's head. The arena is purposely chosen for the pale-faces to be spectators of it, that it may strike terror to their souls, by giving them a foretaste of what is to be their fate. For it is the "*Fandango de crancos*," *anglicé,* scalp-dance.

What they on the mountain first see is some half-score of the savages issuing forth from the *corral* and taking their way to the appointed spot. They bear with them a long pole painted blood-red, recognizable as one of the wagon-tongues, drawn to a sharp point at its inner end. In a trice it is stuck upright in the turf, showing at its top something very different from the chains late there. It is the skin of a human head, with the hair hanging straggled down, light-coloured hair proclaiming it that of a pale-face. They could crown that pole with scores of such scalps, many having their leggings fringed with them. But for the rites of the ceremony to be performed one is deemed sufficient; and to make it more terribly impressive, the one selected shows by the silken gloss of the hair with its luxuriance and length to have been taken from the head of a woman! There are women looking at it now, and young girls of different ages. For all have left the spring and come forward to the viewing-point. It is a sight to inspire them with awe enough of itself, without their being told of a certain and terrible signification attached to the fact of a *woman's* scalp being fixed to the head of that pole instead of a *man's*. Pedro Vicente could make it known to them, but does not.

Ere long the ceremonial of vengeful menace commences, the Indians approaching the ensanguined stake and forming in wide cordon around it; all of them in full war-paint, a fresh coat of it in their garish devices of various colours, scarlet and blood-red predominating. But there is one common to all, a symbol in white — the same borne by him who is sleeping his last sleep in the *corral*. They have but assumed it for the occasion to do honour to their dead chief. And a frightful form of demonstration it is. Over two hundred men, mahogany-coloured savages, all naked to the waist, each with a death's head and crossbones done in white gypsum on the central and prominent portion of his breast! 'T were enough to awe the heart of any one within their reach or in their power, and many of the spectators above tremble at beholding the horrid insignia.

The dance begins, the savages in circle tramping round and round the pole "how-howing" as they go, at first in slow step and with voice barely audible. Soon, however, the one quickens, the other becoming louder, till the step is a violent bounding, the voice raised to highest pitch. Louder and angrier grow the shouts as they turn their eyes upward to the scalp, and still more violent their gesticulations, arms in air with weapons whirled above their heads, till at length several rush at the reddened stake, and hack it down with their tomahawks. Then follows a confused struggle for the scalp, in which it is torn to pieces, all who can appropriating shred or tress, but to spit upon it in vindictive scorn, while still further rending it!

The demoniac dance is now over; some it has most excited come rushing towards the ravine, as though they really meant risking an assault. All above draw back out of sight, only they appointed for the defence staying by the stone artillery. But they are not called upon to hurl any more down just yet. Warned by the event of overnight, the savages think better of it, and before getting too close, come to a stop, and content themselves with wordy threats and a brandishing of weapons.

But, empty and impotent as is their menacing attitude, it makes deep impression on those against whom it is directed. For it tells them they may never more go down that gorge, or set foot upon the plain below, to live an hour, if a minute, after.

CHAPTER XV.

IN the great desert land of Apacheria there are Coyoteros and Coyoteros; some, abject miserable creatures among the lowest forms of humanity; others, men of fine port, courage, and strength—true Indian warriors. Of these is the band of El Cascabel, noted for its frequent hostile expeditions to the settlements of Sonora, as that on which it was bent when brought up by the Lost Mountain. So unexpectedly deprived of its chief, will it continue on that expedition? or lay siege to the party of travelling miners as he intended doing? A question asked the miners themselves of one another, but not after witnessing the scalp-dance. Then knew they for sure that the siege was to be carried out. As further evidence of it, that very afternoon the mules and horses of the caravan are collected into droves, tied head to tail, and conducted away from the ground altogether by a number of Indians placed in charge of them—evidently that there should not be too many mouths on the pastures around the camp, which, though good, are but of limited extent. Only some of the inferior animals, with the beeves, are allowed to remain as provision for the besiegers.

* * * * *

The miners above have meanwhile been busy getting matters regulated in their new camp, or bivouac, soon as convinced that the enemy did not intend assault. All repair thither, only a limited number of videttes keeping post by the gorge. Around the *ojo de agua* is witnessed a scene of curious interest. To the two tents set up on the day before are being added sheds and arbour-like huts, with such haste that ere night all are completed, for the cloud of the

night before, portending rain, still covers the
western sky, though not a drop has yet fallen.

Just as the last of daylight glimmers over
the plain a very drown and downpour, as if to
make up for its long absence. The sky is all
clouded now, but with clouds at short intervals
riven by forking spears of lightning, while the
accompanying thunder is almost continuous.

Under the yellow light the lake glistens as if
it was molten gold, while the rebound upwards
from the heavy drops shows something like a
golden spray hanging all over it. On beyond
the out-going stream, late but a tiny rivulet, has
changed to a foaming torrent, madly breaking
its way across the plain ; while the in-going rill
from the _messas_ summit has become a series of
cascades and cataracts.

The Indians, fearing a stampede by their
horses, draw them in from their picket pins,
hobble, and make them fast round the wheels of
the wagons, but they are still more solicitous
about the fine _caballada_ captured and sent
away ; for nearly every one of these, with all

the mules, has a pack saddle on its back with the distributed dry goods, and other desirable articles not taken up the *messa*. In short, if that pack drove be lost, they may not have much to reward them for the season's raid. They might have sent the wagons along, but aware of the use to which these are often put by the pale-faces, as sleeping-tents, are noting the approach of the storm, and determine to utilize them in similar fashion. That night at least they would need them, and it might be many more.

So, as the rain falls, lightning flashes, and thunder rolls, there is a close-packed crowd under the tilt of each, with the big tent full to its entrance-flap; and still there is not space enough to shield all from that torrent of the sky, a large number retreating under ledges of the cliffs that overhang near by.

The miners are all under shelter; they, too, sure of the approaching storm, having worked hard during the later hours of the day. The *messa* gave them material for wall and roof.

Posts from the indigenous trees with scantling poles cut from saplings of many kinds, and a thatch of *cycas* and other grasslike plants, which abounded on the summit. Men accustomed as they to handling ropes and gearing, were not long in running up a house sufficient for shelter, and now every such domicile is filled to its door-jambs; men, women, and children mingled together, some standing, some seated on the bundles of goods that, but for their being inside, would have been lost. They had thought of that too.

Up to a certain hour the people of quality are all inside one tent, which shows bright from a light burning inside it: their conversation is, of course, about the circumstances which surround them. Who, then, could talk of any other? Don Estevan believes that the killing of the Rattlesnake may be a disadvantage to them rather than otherwise, making the vengeance of his followers more implacable than at least it should do. But he has yet another reason for so believing. In his own military

expeditions he had become acquainted with
El Cascabel's second in command, a sub-chief,
equalling the others in hostility to the whites,
while far excelling him in ability.

But it is too soon yet to discuss such chances.
Rest was the one thing needed; and at the
usual hour for retiring, all, save those detailed
for picket-guard, seek repose.

Just as on the previous night the less ex-
perienced stand the first watches of the night,
keeping the rain off with waterproof *scrapes;*
only at intervals need they look down, and
then, unlike as on the night before, everything is seen as under a meridian sun, for it is
while the lightning gleams they make their
intermittent examination of the gorge path,
cascading stream, trees, and rocks illuminated
by it as by a thousand torches ; only towards
morning do their blazes become less frequent,
gradually dying out as the rain ceases to fall.
Henry Tresillian is again on watch duty, having
insisted upon it, notwithstanding the opposition
made by the others of his party.   But he has a

reason they do not understand—indeed, he has
not communicated it to them; during the earlier
hours of the night he fancied having observed
a dark object far off on the plain, seemingly in
the shape of a horse ; but returning several times
to look, afterwards he could not see it again.
Now, on the post midnight watch, at each blaze
he runs his eye around the spot where he
fancied the dark object to have been, only in
the very last one to see it again, and make sure
it was a horse ; but his ears tell him more than
his eyes, for in the dark spell succeeding the
silence of the elements restored he several times
hears a neigh, which he recognizes as that of
his own horse, Crusader.

And when the day at length dawns he sees
the noble animal itself only a short distance
beyond the lower end of the lake, with head
upraised and muzzle pointed up the gorge, as
though in a morning salute to himself.

CHAPTER XVI.

AN UNLOOKED-FOR ENEMY.

A THRILL of delight sweeps through the heart of the English youth at beholding Crusader in this attitude, as if the horse said, "You see, I 've not forsaken you." Satisfaction also to think the animal capable of making its own way, and finding sustenance in those wilds; for should it ever be their fate to escape from that mountain, there might be a hope of horse and master coming together again. But there is fear commingled with these feelings, this causing the eyes of Henry Tresillian to turn with quick glance towards the left, where a small portion of the camp of the Indians is visible outside the flanking battlements of rock; every moment he expects to see issue from it a

band of dusky horsemen in start for a new
pursuit of his favourite.

Crusader seems to have some anticipation of
the same; he stands restlessly, now glancing up
the chine, anon at the corraled wagons with
hundreds of horses around them. These he
regards suspiciously, being the same with which
he had already declined to associate; perhaps
he may be wondering where are the other
horses, his companions of the caravan? Whether
or no, he hesitates to approach nearer to the old
camping-ground, steadfastly keeping his place.
Where he stands he is so nigh his former
master that the latter might without any difficulty make himself heard, and at first the
English youth had it on the tip of his tongue
to call out a friendly greeting, but quick reflection showed him its imprudence. The very
worst thing he could do for the horse's sake.
Crusader would be sure to recognize his voice
and respond with a neigh, which would awake
a chorus of yells in the Coyoteros' camp, and
at once set the savages on the alert.

For the last half-hour or more the black horse had been quiet, and there were several reasons against his being seen. He was upon the opposite, or western edge of the stream, which had a fringing of reeds and bushes, broken in places, but here and there continuous for yards, and behind one of these clumps he had come to a stand ; even in bright day, as it now nearly is, he would there be invisible to the occupants of the captured camp.

But if only to water their horses, the Indians will soon be dashing down to the lake, and then all chance of his remaining longer unobserved will be at an end.

With gaze more riveted on the horse than ever, for there is something strange in his behaviour, Henry Tresillian watches him with wondering eyes, his heart audibly pulsating. What if they should again get him in a ring, and this time display more adroitness in hurling their laryettes? Crusader might not be so clever on every occasion.

While thus speculating on the result, a noise

reaches the ears of the English youth, as also
of others on vidette post, which causes an
instant and sudden turning of their eyes in the
opposite direction. Many voices, indeed, all
loud and all in excited tone. Voices of men,
shrieks of women, and cries of terrified children,
all coming from one place, their new camp by
the spring.

The videttes stay not on their post an instant
longer, but forsaking it, rush towards *ojo de
agua*. Sounds inexplicable, mysterious! What
can be causing them? The only suggestion
attempted is, that the Indians after all may have
contrived to ascend the *messa* by some secret
path known only to themselves, and are in the
act of attacking from the rear. What other
enemy could cause such a scare? Every voice
in the miners' party is seemingly convulsed with
affright.

The young Englishman dashes on ahead,
tearing through branches, and bounding over
trunks of prostrate trees. Vicente, who had
brought the watch with him, is close behind,

though he has not such stimulus to haste, for amidst the *fracas* of noises, Henry Tresillian hears a sweet voice calling out his own name in a tone of appeal.

Not till they come to the very edge of the glade do they discover the cause of all these wild demonstrations, though something seen an instant or two earlier leads Vicente to conjecture it. Men, but chiefly boys and girls, standing on the branches of trees high as they can climb, as though there to behold some passing spectacle.

" *El orso !*—the grizzly !"

" It must be that," says Vicente, pressing on.

And so it proves. As the videttes so mysteriously summoned in see on getting to the nearer end of the glade which surrounds the spring, at its farther one are two gigantic animals, one a quadruped, the other to all appearances a biped. For all, both are four-footed creatures, and the most dangerous to be encountered in all the desert lands of America. So utterly are they regardless of the odds

against them that they would advance to the
attack of horse or man, even were there twenty
of these together, and have been known to
come shuffling into a well-appointed camp, and
make a grand havoc, ere means may be taken
to destroy or eject them.

The Indian tiger or the African lion are not
more to be dreaded in their jungles than is the
ursus ferox in the districts it specially affects.

Strange that the pair at the inner end of the
glade had not yet shown signs of any determination to assail the camp ; indeed, they seem to
be amusing themselves at the stir their presence
has created, or rather as if making amusement
for the surprised people. He, upon his hams,
for it is the male who has so erected himself,
is playing his fore-paws about, as if engaged in
an act of prestidigitation ; while his mate, at
intervals also rearing up, seems to be playing
the part of juggler's assistant, the whole spectacle being comical in the extreme. The tragical
part of it had not yet commenced, and for two
reasons.

First, that the grizzly bear seldom makes instant attack, appearing to enter on the field of battle more by accident than from any predetermined hostile resolve. Only after shammering about a while, and at intervals uttering a snort till their passions get the better of them, and then woe to man or horse that comes within the hug of their powerful fore-paws! With its enormous curving claws, many inches in length, a grizzly bear has been known to drag the largest ox or horse to the ground, as a terrier would a rabbit.

Henry Tresillian looks only to the two canvas tents to see the señora inside one, her face visible through the opening, while Gertrude is still without by the side of her own father and his. The young girl appears behaving herself more bravely than any of the older people around. She is inspired with fresh courage at the sight of the English youth bounding towards her, gun in hand.

By this time others have got out their guns, and a party led by the *major-domo* is advancing

to fire on the bears.   The *gambusino,* hitherto
not having observed this party, now sees it,
noting its intention.   He would frustrate it, and
makes the attempt, shouting in loudest voice,
" For your lives, don't draw trigger upon them.
They may go without——"

Too late ; his after-words were drowned by
the report of the steward's great gun, and the
male bear came down on all fours, evidently hit,
but as evidently little harmed, his active motions
afterwards telling of a wound he no more regarded than the scratch of a pin.   It perhaps
only tickled him, and his biting at the place
might be but to take the itch out.   It angered
him, though, to the highest pitch, for again
rising on his hind-legs he swung his head about,
snorting continuously, with an occasional scream
which bespoke either pain or vengeance.

There was no sign of intention to retreat on the
part of either male or female, for they seemed
to act in concert and with mutual understanding,
this, in the moment after, impelling them to
forsake their stationary spot and come rushing

on towards the tents and boothies. Showing
motion quick enough now, they are soon in
their midst, the female instantly after seizing a
boy who in fright had fallen from one of the
branches directly in front of her, and killing the
poor lad by a single stroke of her powerful
fore-paw.   He is not unavenged : before she
has time to seek for a second victim the men
with guns gather around her, and regardless of
danger, for their blood is now up, go so close
that some of their muzzles become buried in
her long shaggy fur.   Then the cracks of eight
or ten guns ring out almost simultaneously, and
the she-grizzly comes to ground.

But the male, the more formidable of the
two, is still afoot, and where are the eight or ten
guns to give him his *coup de grâce ?*   Only four
loaded ones are seen in hand, the majority of
the people who have been able to arm themselves, in their haste, not much over a dozen,
having instinctively rushed towards the bear
that was attacking the lad.   But now the other,
having passed that spot, is making for one to be

defended by the four guns in question, that tent inside which are the Señora Villanueva and her daughter. No need to say that the defenders are Don Estevan, Robert Tresillian, his son Henry, and the *gambusino*. A formidable defence, nevertheless, since, in addition to their guns, they carry knives and pistols, the last double-loaded.

They have thrown cloaks and other dark cloths over the tents to make them less conspicuous, but the bear seems imbued by a vindictive determination to attack in that very quarter, and straight towards them comes he.

"Let me fire first, señores," claims Vicente, "and low from my knee my bullets may turn him side-ways, and if so, then your chance, pour in your broadside, aim just behind the shoulder, half-way down."

Saying which the *gambusino* drops on one knee, bringing his gun to his shoulder not an instant too soon, for the huge monster is now within ten feet of him. The sharp but full report, with a tuft of hair seen starting off the

DEATH OF THE GRIZZLY

bear's right neck well back on the shoulder, tells that the animal has been hit there, just as Vicente had intended it, his design being for the others to get flanking shots, which they do, one and all, the bear instantly slewing round as before to bite the wounded spot. This brought his left shoulder to front well spread out, and making the best of marks, into which was simultaneously poured the contents of four barrels with twice as many bullets, hitting so close together as to make an ensanguined irregular disc about the size of a man's hand. No pistols nor knives were needed, no supplementary weapons of any kind, the bear breathing his last ere the reports of the guns had ceased reverberating along the cliffs.

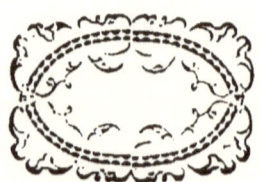

CHAPTER XVII.

THE scene, all action and excitement, has nevertheless occupied but a brief space of time : scarce two minutes since the grizzly bears first showed themselves on the edge of the glade till both lie dead within it—victims of their own ferocity.

It might have been very different, and under like circumstances nearly always is. Many cases are recorded in which half a score of camp travellers have succumbed to the insane rage of a single grizzly. Fortunate, too, had been the miners in their shots—no doubt due to the short range at which they were fired—for the thick, tough skin of this animal is almost ball-proof, and one has been known to bear off a dozen bullets in its body, and carry them about with it afterwards.

The very openness of their danger, with no prospect of escaping it, had lent to the miners the courage of despair, and so made them more fearless in their attack; otherwise they would have fired at the enemy without approaching so near, perhaps to fail. Enough damage has been done notwithstanding, and a cry of lamentation succeeds the shots, and general shouting, as the women gather around the body of that single victim to the fury of the bears. Frightfully mutilated it is, showing parallel tears over the breast—the tracks of claws, all running blood, and a huge gash by the throat where the first stroke had been given.

"*Esta Pablito Rojas !*" cries a voice, identifying the lad, others adding in sympathetic chorus, "*Pobre ! pobre-cci !*"

There is one who takes no part in these demonstrations—Henry Tresillian. He is in fact no longer in the camp, for soon as the second grizzly had been disposed of, he started

back for the vidette post, and so abruptly as
to make all wonder who were observing him.
Among the rest Gertrude herself, who thought
it strange he should not stay to speak some
words of congratulation. He but muttered one
or two, with the name of his horse, well known
to her, and was off.

Now, from his former point of view, he again
beholds Crusader standing just as left, and still
to all appearance unmolested. It is more than
he expected, but there may be reasons: possibly
the shouts and fusillade above have for a time
drawn the attention of the Indians in that direction. This will not be for long, and Crusader's
master but counts the moments till he see him
assailed and chased.

Nor are they many. Just after his return to
the ravine's head he observes nigh threescore
dusky horsemen move out beyond the flanking
embattlement of rock; not hastily, nor in confusion, but in deliberate and long deployed line,
which stretches afar over the *llano*.

Crusader sees them too, and seems to regard

them with indifference; he has taken to browsing on a piece of rich pasture lying along the stream's edge, this alone for the time occupying him. That he is the objective point of their movement is evident, though none of them are heading straight towards him, their design being evidently to get around him.

After all, is he going to let himself be surrounded, and approached in this easy manner? Such is the interrogatory which passes among those watching from above, for the videttes have returned to their post, with others accompanying them.

One answers it, saying, "It's not at all likely. He let himself be taken in a trap! More like the red-skins will find themselves in one before long. See! they begin to find it now!"

This, from Pedro Vicente in his old spirit, as he points to the line of savages far extended.

The files have by this faced westward, but are advancing towards the stream; now, on nearing it, they are seen to stop abruptly as if in surprise. Then, after an instant, all wheel

round and ride back eastward, till getting on
their old line, they return at a gallop towards
their camp. They have discovered the stream
to be impassable.

"That horse is the *demonio* himself," says
Pedro Vicente—"neither more nor less. He
must have known they could not cross the
swollen streamlet, or he'd never have stopped
by it as he has done. But they've not given
him up yet. No! see: they're going round
by the head of the lake."

Just this they intend, as is seen by their
advancing towards the point where the lake
commences by the mouth of the ravine. They
have no difficulty in crossing its in-going
stream, a few minutes after the rain ceased
having reduced this to its normal condition of
a tiny rivulet.

And like some dark, disagreeable vision
Henry Tresillian sees pass before his eyes the
savage cohort, file after file, one disappearing
after another, till at length no animated form
is observable on the plain below, save that

their eyes have been hitherto regarding with interest.

There is a long interval without event; nearly an hour elapses ere Crusader shows any sign, his head almost continuously to the grass, raised only occasionally, as he changes place upon it. All this time the Indians are out of sight, with no sound coming from the direction they had taken.

But at length there is a sound, a startled neigh from the black horse, who, tossing his crest in air, rears upward with a curving sweep, and then darts straight away, as if in flight from an advancing enemy — the enemy seen instantly afterwards as several mounted men disclose themselves from the western framework of rock, all in a tail-on-end gallop.

Crusader has taken along the edge of the stream, and follows it in parallel direction downwards, just as he fled before from the same pursuers. There would seem no chance of their overtaking him now; for he appears to gain distance at every bound, without even straining himself. But lo! what is that?

"*Santos Dios !* They've headed him. *Milraya !* what a pity!"

It is the *gambusino* who thus exclaims, seeing other horsemen on the plain farther points on, all facing towards the stream, evidently to in-intercept the chased steed.

Crusader sees them too, for he is now close up to them; but forsaking the course he has hitherto followed, he makes an abrupt turn and breaks off westward, continuing this direction in full gallop, till the rocks hide him from view.

Alike the pursuers thrown round, pass out of sight one after another, and again that part of the *llano* resumes its wonted aspect of stern, savage tranquillity.

For most of those composing the party of spectators the chase had no particular interest, and only a few of them were gathered around the point where it could be viewed. Indeed, but a few heard of Crusader being seen, the greater and more serious event obscuring that of lesser note. And now these few, one after the other, again go back to *ojo de agua*, to take part in the duties of the day.

But the English youth still stays by the vidette post, with eye constantly directed on the plain below, and ears listening intently, to catch any sound that may come from the western side; apprehensively, too, for he fears to hear shots.

The savages failing to catch the black horse with their laryettes, may spitefully endeavour to bring him down with their guns. This, indeed, is the real danger his young master has been dreading, and which for the time engrosses all his thoughts.

Luckily not for long. Within less than an hour the dusky horsemen, in twos and threes, come straggling back across the open ground between the lake's head and their camp, so continuing till the last of them have returned, all with discomfited air, but none with Crusader as their captive. And as no report of gun has been heard, it is more than probable he has once more eluded them.

CHAPTER XVIII.

THE exciting events above recorded, as occurring in quick succession, are followed by a period of repose lasting for days. Alike reigns it on the mountain summit and around its base; in the camp of the besieged as of the besiegers.

Withal, in the latter there is no lack of activity; parties go and come at all hours, but more especially during those of the night. Scouts sent out; it may be for many purposes. But one large detail is observed on a certain day to make the complete round of the mountain, every here and there halting with front towards it, as if for minute examination of its cliffs from base to summit; evidently to be satisfied whether there be any possible chance for the white men to reach the plain otherwise than down that chine cut by the watercourse.

While making this *reconnaisance* they have been narrowly watched by eyes from above, and as no particular point has been observed to attract their attention, it is concluded that they deem their pale-faced prisoners quite secure, only calling for a little patience ere they may evidently lay hands on them.

The same movement also gives assurance to their intended victims, but of a kind not so satisfactory. It tells them how determined their enemy is, how retentive his grasp, and implacable his vengeance. All this with no increased hope on their part of being able to escape him. Thought of how has not yet taken shape in their minds. How could it? So many present facts and fears engrossing them, they have found little time to reflect on the future.

And a new fear has now arisen which calls for steps to be taken. There may be other grizzly bears on the *mesa*, and if so these monsters will be prowling around the camp to assail it at any instant. Better they be met outside at a distance off, there attacked, and if possible exterminated.

This conclusion come to, Don Estevan gives orders for all to arm, and a general *battue* is made over the summit of the Cerro. Paths are hacked through the underwood everywhere, laying open many a spot never before trodden by foot of man. Strange birds are flushed from their nests, and strange animals are seen stealing away through the thick tangle of *llianas*, chiefly of the reptilian order, as armadillos, lizards, the curious horned frog *(Agama cornuta)*, and serpents—most numerous of all that whose retreat is marked by the defiant rattle which has given it its name. Scores of *cascabelés* are started out of the dead leaves and branches, their vibratory "skirr" resounding everywhere.

But quadrupeds turn up as well. At intervals the crack of gun tells of one shot at, whether killed or no. Now a wild sheep, now a prong-horn antelope, or it may be but a hare or rabbit. The great wolf is also found there, and his lesser and more cowardly congener, the coyote; but no more bears—grizzly or other—nor sign of them. Evidently the two killed at the camp were the sole monarchs of the mountain.

The day's hunt, for it occupied a whole day, gives satisfaction in more ways than one. First, by doing away with all apprehension of danger from *Ursus ferox;* secondly, by affording a plentiful supply of present food ; and, thirdly, in there being still more on the mountain, giving proof of the abundance of them.

Nor is the vegetable element lacking, but present in all its varieties of root, fruit, and berry. The *mezcal,* whose baked stem forms staple food for their enemies, grows on the *mesa.* Its use is known to the *gambusino,* as others of the miners. Several sorts of *mezquite* trees are found there, whose long pendulous *siliques* contain seeds which can be ground into a meal making nutritious bread, while the cones of the edible pine (*Pinus edulis*) — "*piñon-*

nuts" as called—are in quantity all around. For fruit there are several varieties of the cactus, with that of pear-shape, and all the rich juiciness of a pear, the famed *pitathaya*. In short, the Cerro Perdido is a very oasis, its cornucopœia peculiar to the desert. With so bountiful a supply of provisions the besieged need not fear famine, at least for a long time. Their resources, carefully husbanded, may last for weeks.

And on time rests their only hope; their sole chance of being rescued depending on that, by some means or other, their situation may become known to their friends at Arispe, or their countrymen elsewhere.

But what likelihood of this? As already stated, the Lost Mountain is out of the line of all travel and traffic. Months, a year, nay, years may elapse ere a wayfarer of any kind stray to it, or near it. So their chances of being seen there by friendly eyes, to say naught of their position being understood, are as those of castaways on a desert isle in mid-ocean.

And as shipwrecked men they hoist signals of distress. Any one approaching that solitary eminence from the south might wonder to see a flag floating from a tall staff over its southern end, giving it all the greater resemblance to a fortress with banner waving above. A tricolour flag, bearing the symbolic badge of the Mexican Republic—the Eagle upon the Nopal! It is that Don Estevan had meant to have erected over the new mine, now little likely ever to be displayed there. For now it is unfolded to tell a tale of threatening disaster, and attract the eyes of those who may do something to avert it.

But for this dark uncertainty of future there is nothing irksome, not even disagreeable, in their present life. On the contrary, it might be even called pleasant; plenty to eat, plenty to drink, sufficient freedom of range, a sapphire sky above, with an atmosphere around them whose heat is tempered by breezes ever blowing, ever laden with the fragrance of fruit and flower.

And no scene of sombre gloomy silence; instead, one enlivened by the notes of many wild warblers, both diurnal and nocturnal. By day the jarring yet cheering cry of the blue jay and the red cardinal; the mewing of the cat-bird, or the "hew-hew" of hawk in pursuit of his victim. By night, the more melodious, all incomparable song of the *czentzontlé*—mocking-bird of Mexico—oft intermingled with another song, but little less powerful or sweet, that of the *cuitlacoche*—a second species of New World nightingale, not so well known.

Life in the odd aërial camp now settles down into a sort of routine, each day having its separate calls and duties. The watch is, of course, kept up, and with no falling off in its vigilance. For although the besiegers have not again shown any sign of an intention to try the assault, who knows what may be in the mind of these subtle savages?

Only at night need there be any fear, and only when it is darkest. At other times the vidette duty is a matter of easy fulfilment.

In truth the miners might almost fancy themselves in picnic, having a happy time of it, halfway between earth and heaven. But they are not there by choice, too well knowing its stern necessity. And this, with the dark doubtful future, robs them of all zest for enjoyment. So the hours pass not merrily, but wearily.

CHAPTER XIX.

WHO TO BE THE FORLORN HOPE?

DAY succeeds day with no brightening of hopes to those beleagured on the Lost Mountain. Instead, in each something arises to make their prospects darker, if that were possible.

About ten days after the commencement of the siege the besiegers have their force increased, a fresh party coming down from the north, evidently in obedience to a summons, which they who drove off the captured *caballada* have carried back. But for what purpose this accession of strength, when it is not needed? They on the ground are already enough, and to spare.

The miners cannot guess what they have come about, unless it be the remaining braves of the tribe, to take part in some ceremony

over their fallen chief, or be present when the
time arrives for the wreaking of vengeance.

It has nothing to do with that, however;
solely a conception of their new leader, El
Zopilote, who has his reasons for carrying out
the raid down the Horcasitas. So on the
second day after, the besieging party, instead
of being one hundred men the more, is all that
the less; at least two hundred seen to issue
forth from the camp, and proceed southward in
full war-paint and panoply, with all their frightful
insignia. As successive files they move off
along the stream's edge, it might seem as some
gigantic serpent commencing its crawl towards
prey. And many on the mountain, with a
suspicion of where they are going, have a pity-
ing heart for those who live on the banks of
the lower Horcasitas.

Enough, however, to think of themselves,
and each hour more than enough; for as the
days pass circumstances present a still sterner
front. The supply of provisions, at first seeming
inexhaustible, proves to have a limit. There

are over seventy mouths to feed, which calls for a large daily quantity. So one by one the wild quadrupeds give out, the birds long before these, frightened by the constant chase and fusillade, forsaking the place altogether. The store of *tasajo* and other preserved meats begins to be drawn upon. When these come to an end, so too must all the suspense, all the agonies of that quaint, quasi imprisonment, to terminate in real captivity, or indeed death itself.

In the tent of Don Estevan some seven or eight of the mining people are assembled; the two *dueños* are of course present, with the *mayor-domo*, the chief engineer, and other heads of departments. No need to say the *gambusino* is among them. They are there to take counsel on the events of the day, and the means of the morrow. Every night it has been their custom to do so, and on this one—for it is at night—there is nothing very different to speak of from any other.

Still, Don Estevan has conceived a thought

which had not hitherto occurred to him, and now lays it before the assembled conclave.

"*Caballeros!* I can think of only one way—poor, doubtful chance it is—by which we may get rescued. Some one must contrive to pass their sentries."

"Impossible!" is the thought of all hearing him, one or two expressing it in speech. For of all the things observed as vigorously kept up, never relaxed for an hour—even a moment—has been that sentinel line thrown across the plain from flank to flank of the ravine. All day long it has appeared there, and all through the night evidently redoubled.

"Pity if it be," rejoins Don Estevan, yielding to what appears the general sentiment. "And to think that one word at Arispe would make all well. My own brother-in-law, Colonel Requenes, in command there with a regiment of lancers—they of Zacatecas. In less than half an hour they could be in the saddle, and hastening to our relief. *Ay Dios!* if we can't communicate with them we are lost—surely lost!"

At this, Robert Tresillian says, interrogatively:

"I wonder how many of our people could find the way back to Arispe?"

Without altogether comprehending what he means, several numbers are mentioned in a guessing way, according to the estimate of each. Pedro Vicente thinks at least thirty could,—certainly all the *arrieros* and *vaqueros*.

"What is your idea, Don Roberto?" at length asks the senior partner.

"That all of those who know the way back be mustered, and two taken from them by lot, who will run the risk of passing the Indian sentries. If they succeed, then all may be saved; if on the contrary, it will be but to lose their lives a little sooner. I propose that all submit to the lottery—all who are unmarried."

"I agree with the Señor Tresillian," here puts in the *gambusino*. "Some of us must contrive to get past them at whatever risk. For my part, I'm willing to be one, with any other."

The generous proposal is received with applause, but not accepted,—it would not be fair; and in fine it is agreed upon, that fate shall determine who shall be the pair to run the proposed risk—the ceremony for deciding it to take place on the morrow.

In the morning it comes off soon as breakfast is eaten. All known to be eligible are summoned together on a spot of ground apart, and told the purport of their being so assembled. No one objects, or tries to evade the dangerous conscription; instead, there are even some who, like Vicente, would volunteer for the duty.

For is not one of the *dueños*—the brave Englishman and his son, there present—both offering themselves as candidates like any of the common men?

No volunteering, then, is allowed; fortune alone permitted to decide on whom shall be the forlorn hope.

The quaint lottery, though awe-inspiring, occupies but a brief space of time. Against the number of men who are to take part in it, a like number of *piñon*-nuts have been counted out, and dropped into a deep-crowned *sombrero.* Two of the nuts have been already stained with gunpowder, the others left in their natural colour; but no one by the feel could tell which was which. The black ones are to be the *prizes.*

The men stand in a ring round Don Estevan, with another who is among the exempt in the centre. These hold the hat, into which one after another, stepping from the circle, led forward blindfolded, inserts his hand, and draws out a nut. If white, he goes clear; but long before the white ones are exhausted the two blacks are taken up, which brings the ceremony to an abrupt end, that deciding all.

They who have drawn the *prizes* are a muleteer and a cattle drover, both brave fellows. They had need be, for this very night they will have to run the gauntlet of life and death, perhaps ere the morrow's sun to be no more.

CHAPTER XX.

A FATAL FAILURE.

IT is a day of anxious solicitude. If the night turn out a dark one, the messengers whom fate has chosen for the perilous enterprise are to set out on their errand. They know it is to be a moonless one, but for all, in the diaphanous atmosphere of that upland plateau, it may be too clear to make the passing of the Indian sentinels at all possible.

The afternoon begets hope : a bank of heavy clouds is seen rising along the western sky, which, rolling higher and higher, brings on a downpour of rain. It is of short continuance, however—over before sunset, the clouds again dispersing. Then the darkness comes down, but for a long time only in a glimmering of grey, the stars in grand sheen making it almost as clear if there was moonlight.

The sentinels can be seen in their old places like a row of dark stakes, conspicuous against the green turf on which they are stationed. They are at short distances apart, and every now and then forms are observed moving from one to the other, as if to keep them continuously on the alert.

So thus, nigh up to the hour of midnight, and the miners begin to despair of their messengers being able to pass out—at least, on this night.

But soon, to their satisfaction, something shows itself promising a different result. The surface of the lake has suddenly turned white, as if under a covering of snow. It is fog. Through the heated atmosphere the lately-fallen rain is rising in vapour, and within its misty shroud it envelopes not only the lake, but the plain around its edges. It rolls over the line of savage watchers, on up between the jaws of the chine, till in its damp clammy film it embraces the bodies of those who are waiting above.

" Now 's your time, *muchachos !* " says Don Estevan, addressing himself to those who are to adventure. "There could not be a better opportunity; if they can't be passed now, they never can."

The two men are there ready, and equipped for the undertaking. Young fellows both, with a brave look, and no sign of quailing or desire to back out. Each carries a small wallet of provisions strapped to his person, with a pistol in his belt, but no other arms or accoutrements to encumber them. In subtleness and activity, more than mere physical force, lie their chances of success.

A shaking of hands with such of their old comrades as are near, farewells exchanged when they pass over the parapet of loose stones to commence the descent, with many a "*va con Dios!*" sent after them in accents of earnest prayerfulness. Then follows an interregnum of profound silence, during which time they at the ravine's head listen with keenest anxiety.

After a few seconds a slight rustling below tells that one of the two has made a slip, or pushed a stone out of place; but nothing comes

of it. Then a horse neighs in the distant camp,
and soon after another, neither of them having
any significance.   No more the screaming of
wild-fowl at the lower end of the lake, nor the
querulous cry of "chuck-will's widow," hawking
high over it.   None of these sounds have any
portent as to the affair in hand, and they, listening, begin to hope that it has succeeded—for
surely there has been time for the two men to
have got beyond the guarded line?

Hope premature, alas! to be disappointed.
Up out of the mist comes the sound of voices,
as if in hail, followed by dubious response, and
quick succeeding a struggle with shots.   Then
a cry or two as in agony, a shout of triumph,
and all silent as before.

*   *   *   *   *

For the rest of the night they on the *mesa*
sleep not.   Too surely has their scheme failed,
and their messengers fallen victims to it.   If
they were any doubts about this, these are set
at rest at an early hour of the morning.

Sad evidence they have to convince them.

On the spot where the scalp dance had taken place a red pole is again erected, as the other ornamented with the skins of human heads. But not now to be danced around; though for a time they, looking from above, think there is to be a repetition of that savage ceremony. Soon they are undeceived, and know it to be a spectacle still more appalling. From the camp they see a man conducted, whom they identify as one of their ill-fated messengers. Taken on to the stake, he is placed back against it, with arms extended and strapped to a cross-piece, in a way representing the figure of the Crucifixion. His breast has been stripped bare, and on it is seen painted in white the hideous symbol of the Death's head and cross-bones.

For what purpose all this display? the spectators conjecture among themselves. Not long till they have the answer. They see several scores of the savages range themselves at a certain distance off, each gun in hand, one after the other taking aim and discharging his piece at the human target. Gradually the disc on

the breast is seen to darken, turning red, till at
length not a spot of white is visible.   But long
ere this the head of the hapless victim, drooped
over his shoulder, tells that he is dead.

The cruel tragedy is repeated, showing now
what was not known before, that both the ill-
starred couriers had been taken alive.   He
brought forth next is recognizable, by the picturesque dress still on his person, as the *vaquero*.
But when taken up to the stake he is stripped
of it, the velveteen *jaqueta* pulled from off his
shoulders, his shirt torn away, leaving his breast
bare.   Then with a hurried touch, the grim,
ghastly device is limned upon him, and he is
taken up to the pole as the other.

A fresh fusillade commences, the white gradually showing dimmer, till at length it is deeply
incrimsoned, and the *vaquero* is a lifeless corpse.

When it is all over, the Coyoteros turn towards the gorge, and looking up, give utterance
to wild yells of triumph, brandishing their
weapons in a threatening manner, as much as
to say, "That's the way we'll serve you all,
when the time comes."

A CRUEL TRAGEDY.—p.

CHAPTER XXI.

A PRODIGIOUS LEAP.

NEEDLESS to say that the failure of their scheme with such fatal consequence has deepened the gloom in the minds of the besieged miners, already dark enough. Now more than ever do they believe themselves doomed. There seems no alternative left but surrender or starvation and as both are alike certain death, they dwell not on the first. True, starvation is not yet so close at hand; they have still provisions—some of the old caravan stores—sufficient for a couple of weeks, if carefully served out, while the live stock furnished by the *mesa* itself has not all been exhausted. Some animals as yet remain uncaptured, though how many they know not.

To make sure, another grand *battue* is set on foot to embrace the whole summit area. Every outlying corner and promontory are quartered and beaten, so that no four-footed creature could possibly be there without being seen or shot. The result is a bag, of but small dimensions, though with large variety; a prong-horn antelope, the last of a band that had been daily getting thinned; several sage hares, a wolf, and three or four coyotes. More of these last were startled, but not killed, as they have lairs in the ledges of the cliffs to which they betake themselves, secure from pursuit of hunter.

While the *battue* is at its height, one large quadruped is put up which more than any other excites the ardour of those engaged. It is a big-horn, or Rocky Mountain sheep, remnant of that flock first found upon the *mesa* by Vicente and Henry Tresillian; it is also a ram, a young one, but with grand curvature of horns. One after another all the rest have been made mutton of, and their bones lie bleaching around the camp; but, though several times chased, this sole survivor has ever contrived to escape, as though it had a charmed life. And now again it seems still under such protection; for at starting several shots are fired at it, none taking effect; and it bounds on, apparently unharmed, towards an outlying projection of the plateau.

Those who have emptied their guns follow without staying to re-load; for they form a line which, deployed crossways, cannot fail to enclose and cut off its retreat, making escape impossible. In fine, they effect this purpose; some, with guns still charged, confidently advancing to give the animal its *coup de grâce.* They are even aiming at it, when, lo! a leap upward and outward, with head bent down as one making a dive, and the big-horn bounds over the cliff.

Five hundred feet fall—shattered to atoms on the rocks below!—this their thought as they approach the precipice to see the prodigious leap that must have been taken by the animal in its panic of fear. One, however, draws nigh with a different thought, knows there was method in that seeming madness, and that the *carnero* sprang over with a design. Pedro Vicente it is; and with the others soon upon

the cliff's brow, and, gazing below, to their surprise they see no sheep there, dead and crushed
as expected.   Instead, a live one out upon the
llano, making off in strides long and vigorous.

Sure of its being the same they had just
driven over, all are astounded, expressing their
astonishment in loud ejaculations.   Alone the
gambusino is silent, a pleased expression perva-
ding his countenance, for that extraordinary feat
of the horned creature has let a flood of light
into his mind, giving him renewed hope that
they may still be saved.   He says nothing of
it to those around, leaving it for more mature
consideration, and to be discussed in their
council of the night.

But long after the others have returned to
camp he lingers on the cliff, treading backwards
and forwards along its crest, surveying it from
every possible point of vantage, as though in an
endeavour to find out how the sheep made that
extraordinary descent.

*   *   *   *   *

Another night is on, and, as is their wont, the

chief men of those besieged are assembled in
the tent of Don Estevan. Not discouraged
yet, for there is a rumour among them that
some new plan has been thought of for passing
the Indian sentries, less likely to be disastrous
than that which has failed. It has been the
whisper of the afternoon, their guide being
regarded as he who has conceived a scheme.

When all are together Don Estevan calls
upon him to declare it, saying,

"I understand, Señor Vicente, you've thought
of a way by which a messenger may yet elude
the vigilance of their sentries, and get beyond
them ?"

"I have, your worship."

"Please make it known."

"Nothing more simple; and I only wonder
at not having thought of it before. After all,
that would have been useless, for only this day
have I discovered the thing to be possible."

"We long to hear what it is."

"Well, then, señores, it's but to give them
the slip. Going out by the back door, while

they are so carefully guarding the front.   That
can be done by our letting one down the cliff—
two, if need be."

" But where ? "

" Where the *carnero* went over."

"What ! five hundred feet ?   Impossible !
We have not rope enough to reach half the
distance."

" We don't need rope to reach much more
than a third of it."

" Indeed !   Explain yourself, Don Pedro."

" I will, your worship, and it is thus.   I 've
examined the cliff carefully, where the sheep
went over.   There are ledges at intervals; it is
true not wide, but broad enough for the animal
to have dropped upon and stuck.   They can
cling to the rocks like squirrels or cats.   Some
of the ledges run downwards, then zigzag into
others, also with a downward slope ; and the
ram must have followed these, now and then
making a plunge, where it became necessary, to
alight on his hoofs or horns, as the case might
be.   Anyhow, he got safe to the bottom, as

we know, and where it went down, so may we."

There is a pause of silence, all looking pleased, for the words of the *gambusino* have resuscitated hopes that had almost died out. They can see the possibility he speaks of, their only doubt and drawback being the fear they may not have rope enough.

"It seems but a question of that," says Don Estevan, as if speaking reflectingly to himself.

The others are also considering, each trying to recall how much and how many of their trail ropes were brought up in that hasty *debendade* from their camp below.

"*Por Dios !* your worship," rejoins the *gambusino*, "it is no question of that whatever. We have the materials to make cords enough, not only to go down the cliff, but all round the mountain. Miles, if it were needed!"

"What materials ?" demanded several of the party, mystified.

"*Mira !*" exclaims the *gambusino*. "This !"

He starts up from a bundle of dry *mezcal-*

leaves on which he has been seated, pushing it before him with his foot.

All comprehend him now, knowing that the fibre of these is a flax, or rather hemp, capable of being worked into thread, cloth, or cordage; and they know that on the *mesa* is an unlimited supply of it.

"No question of rope, *caballeros;* only the time it will take us to manufacture it. And with men such as you, used to such gearing, that should not be long."

"It shall not," respond all. "We'll work night and day till it be done."

"One day, I take it, will be enough—that to-morrow. And if luck attend us, by this time to-morrow night we may have our messengers on the way, safe beyond pursuit of these accursed red-skins."

Some more details are discussed maturing their plans for the rope-making. Then all retire to rest, this night with more hopeful anticipations than they have had for many preceding.

CHAPTER XXII.

A YOUTHFUL VOLUNTEER.

ANOTHER day dawns, and as the earliest rays of the sun light up the Cerro Perdido, an unusual bustle is observed in the camp of the besieged. Men are busy collecting the leaves of the *mezcal*-plant, those that are withered and dry from having their corms cut out days before; fortunately there are many of these lying all around. Other men, armed with rudely-shaped mallets, beat them against the trunks of trees, to separate the fibre from the now desiccated pulp; while still others are twisting this into threads, by a further process to be converted into thick ropes.

It is found that after all not so much will be needed; several lassoes had been brought up, tied round the bundles of goods; and with these

197

and other odds and ends of cordage, a rope can be put together full two hundred feet in length, strong enough to sustain the weight of any man. So, long before night the lowering apparatus is ready, and, as before, they await the darkness to make use of it.

Meanwhile Don Estevan, the two Tresillians, and Vicente spend most of the morning on the cliff where the big-horn went over, surveying it from every possible point, taking the bearings of its ledges, and estimating their distances from one another. They are, as the *gambusino* had represented them, a succession of very narrow benches, but wide enough for a man to find footing; some horizontal, others with a slope downwards, then a zigzag bringing them lower, till within a hundred feet from the cliff's base the *façade* of rocks shows sheer and clear. Down to this point all will be easy; and beyond it they anticipate little difficulty, now that they are sure of having sufficient rope.

While engaged in their reconnaissance, an object comes under their eyes which they gaze upon with interest. They are upon the western side of the *mesa* not far above its southern point, the plain on that side being invisible from the camp of the besiegers; and on this, at the distance of a mile or more, there is a spot of pasture due to a tiny rivulet, which, filtering off from the side of the lake, becomes dispersed over a considerable surface, which it moistens and makes green.

Moving to and fro over this verdant stretch is the object which has caught their attention— a horse of large size and coal-black colour, which they know to be no other than Crusader. They are not surprised at seeing him there. Habitually he frequents this spot, which has become his accustomed pasturing-ground, and more than once had Henry Tresillian stood on that cliff regarding him with fond affectionate gaze; more than once, too, had the Indians again gone in chase of him, to be foiled as before. There is he still unlassoed, free of limb as the antelopes seen flitting over the *llano* around him.

After completing the examination of their precipice, and noting all details that may be needed to help out their design, they stand for a time gazing at the horse, his young master with a thought in his mind which he witholds from the others. Nor does he communicate it to them till after their return to the camp, and the question comes up, who are the ones to be lowered down; for it is thought better that two messengers should be sent, as company and support to each other. That is the question to be decided, and up to this hour all expect it to be as before—by lottery.

In fine, when the time arrives for settling it, and the eligible ones are again assembled for drawing lots, a proposal is made which takes every one present by surprise. It comes from the youngest of the party, Henry Tresillian, who says :

"Let me go alone."

All eyes turn upon him inquiringly and in wonder, none more than those of his father, who exclaims:

"You go alone, my son! Why do you propose that?"

"Because it will be best, father."

"How best? I do not understand you."

"Crusader can only carry one."

"Ah! Crusader—that's what you're thinking of?"

"*Por Dios!*" exclaims the senior partner, "I see what your son means, Don Roberto; his idea is admirable!"

"Yes," says the English youth in answer to his father; "I've been thinking of it ever since yesterday. On Crusader's back I can be at Arispe days before any foot messenger could arrive there. Once I had him between my legs, no fear of Indians overtaking me."

"The very thing!" cries Don Estevan, delighted. "But, Señor Henrique, are you sure you can catch the horse?"

"Catch him! he will come to my call. Once on the plain, and within hearing of my voice, I've no fear of his soon being by my side."

"But why not let me take him?" puts in

Pedro Vicente, as if to spare the generous youth from undertaking such a risk. " I know the road better than you, *muchacho.*"

" That may be," returns the other. " But I know it well enough. Besides, Crusader will let no one catch him but myself—much less ride him."

During all this conversation the bystanders regard the young Englishman with looks of admiration. Never before have they seen so much courage combined with intelligence. And all to be exerted in their favour ; for they have not forgotten the fate of their two comrades, put to death in such a cruel fashion. Every one of them fears that the like may befall himself, should it be his ill luck to draw a black *piñon* out of the *sombrero.*

Not the least in admiration is Robert Tresillian himself: his heart swells with pride at the gallant bearing of the boy, his own son, worthy of the ancestral name ; and when Don Estevan turns to him to ask whether he objects to the proposal, it is to receive answer :

"On the contrary, I approve of it. Foot messengers might not reach in time, if at all. My brave boy will do it if it can be done; it may be the means of bringing rescue to us all. If he fail, then I, like the rest of you, must submit to fate."

"I'll not fail," cries the impetuous youth, rushing forward and throwing his arms round his father. "Fear not. I have a belief that God's hand is in it, else why should my noble horse have stayed? Why is he still there?"

"*Virgen santissima!*" exclaims Don Estevan in devout tone. "It would even seem so. Let us hope and pray that the Almighty's hand is in it. If so, we shall be saved."

Henry Tresillian is the hero of the hour, though he has been a favourite with the people of the caravan all along, doing kind offices to this one and that one, helping all who needed help. But now, when they hear he has volunteered on this dangerous service, as it were offering up his life for theirs, encomiums are loud on all sides. Women fall upon their knees, and, with crucifix in hand, offer up prayers for his protection. But Gertrude? Oh, the sad thoughts—the utter woe that strikes through her heart—when she hears tidings of what is intended! She receives them with a wild cry, almost a shriek, with arms outstretched staggering to the side of her mother for support.

"Mamma, father must not let him go. He will be lost, and then—then——"

"Have no fear. Think, *hija mia*, we may all be lost if he do not."

"But why cannot some other go in his place? There are many who know the way as well as he, and that brave *gambusino*, I'm sure, would be willing."

"No doubt he would, dearest; there's some reason against it I do not quite understand. We shall hear all soon, when father returns to the tent."

They do hear the reason; but not any the more to reconcile Gertrude. The young girl is half beside herself with grief, utterly indifferent as to who may observe it. The bud of her love has bloomed into a flower, and she recks not that all the world know her heart is Henry Tresillian's. The cousin left behind at Arispe, supposed to be an aspirant to her hand, is forgotten. All are forgotten, save the one now near, so soon to be cruelly torn away from her. Neither the presence of her father and mother, nor that of his father, restrain her in her wild ravings. She knows she has their approval of her partiality, and her young heart, innocent of guile, yields to nature's promptings.

Her appeals are in vain : what must be must be, and she at length resigns herself to the inevitable. For Henry himself tells her how it is, and that no one possibly could take his place.

It is in dialogue between them, just as the twilight begins to cast its purple shadows over the plain. For the time is drawing nigh for action, and the two have gone apart from the camp to speak the last words of leave-taking. They stand under a tree, hands clasped, gazing into each other's eyes, those of the young girl full of tears.

"*Querida*," he says, "do not weep. 'T will be all well yet—I feel sure of it."

"Would that I could feel so, Henrique; but, oh! dearest, such danger! And if the cruel savages capture you. *Ay Dios!* to think of what they did with the others!"

"Let them catch me if they can. They never will if I once get alongside Crusader. On his back I may defy them."

"True, I believe it. But are you sure of getting upon his back? In the darkness you may not find him."

"If not, it will be but to return to the cliff and be drawn up again."

This assurance somewhat tranquillizes her. There is at least the hope, almost certainty, he will not, as the others, be sacrificed to a fruitless attempt; and, so trusting, she says in conclusion:

"Go, then, *querido mio.* I will no more oppose it, but pray all night long for your safety. I see now it is for the best, and feel that the blessed Mary, mother of God, will listen to my prayers."

No longer hands clasped, but arms entwined, and lips meeting in a kiss of pure holy affection, sanctified by parental consent. Then they return to the camp, where the final preparations are being made for that venture upon which so much depends.

CHAPTER XXIII.

A RIDE IN MID-AIR.

It turns out just such a night as was wished for—moonless, still not obscurely dark. Too much darkness would defeat the end in view. They need light for the lowering down, a thing that will take some time with careful management.

But the miners are the very men for such purpose. Not one of them who has not dangled at a rope's end in a shaft hundreds of feet sheer down into the earth. To them it is habitude—child's play — as to him who spends his life scaling sea-coast cliffs for the eggs and young of birds.

It is yet early when the party entrusted with the undertaking assemble on the edge of the precipice, at the point where the daring adventurer is to make descent. Some carry coils of rope, others long poles notched at the end for fending the line off the rocks, while the *gambusino* is seen bearing a burden which differs from all the rest. A saddle and bridle it is; · his own, cherished for their costliness, but now placed at the service of his young friend, to do what he will with them.

"I could ride Crusader without them," says the English youth : "guide him with my voice and knees; but these will make it surer, and I thank you, Señor Vicente."

"Ah, *muchacho!* if they but help you, how glad 't will make me feel! If they're lost, it wouldn't be for that I 'd grudge the twenty *doblones* the saddle cost me. I 'd give ten times as much to see you seated in it on the *plaza* of Arispe."

" I 'll be there, *amigo*, in less than sixty hours if Crusader hasn't lost his strength by too long feeding on grass."

" I fancy you need not fear that, señorito ; your horse is one that nothing seems to affect.

14

I still cling to the belief he's the devil himself."

"Better believe him an angel—our good angel now, as I hope he will prove himself."

This exchange of speech between the two who have long been *compagnons de chasse,* is only an interlude occurring while the ropes are being uncoiled and made ready.

Instead of a loop to be passed around the adventurer's body, a very different mode for his making descent has been prearranged. He is to take seat in the saddle, just as though it were on the back of a horse, and, with feet in the stirrups and hands clutching the cords that suspend it, be so let down. A piece of wood passed under the tree, and firmly lashed to pommel and cantle, will secure its equilibrium.

Finally all is ready, and, the daring rider taking his seat, is soon swinging in mid-air. Hand over hand they lower him down, slowly, cautiously, listening all the while for a signal to be sent up. This they get in due time—a low whistle telling them that he has reached the first ledge, though they could tell it by the strain upon the rope all at once having ceased.

Up it is drawn again, its owner himself, in turn, taking seat in it, to be lowered down as the other. Then again and again it is hoisted up and let down, till half a score of the miners, stalwart men, Robert Tresillian among them, stand on the bench below.

Now the saddle is detached and fastened on to another rope, when the same process is repeated; and so on, advantage being taken of the sloping ledges, till the last is arrived at.

Here it is but a repetition of what has gone before, only with a longer reach of rope; and here Pedro Vicente takes last leave of the youth who has become so endeared to him.

In the eye of the honest *gambusino* there is that not often seen there, a tear. He flings his arms around the English youth, exclaiming:

"*Dios te guarda, muchacho valiente!* (God guard you, my brave lad)."

The parting between the two is almost as affectionate as that between Henry and his father, the last saying, as he enfolds his son in his arms:

"God go with you, my noble boy!"

In another moment the daring youth is once more in the saddle, going down, down, till he feels his feet upon the plain. Then stepping out of it, and sending up the preconcerted signal, he detaches saddle and bridle from the cords, leaving the latter to swing free.

Shouldering the horse gear with other *impedimenta*, he looks round to get his bearings, and, soon as satisfied about these, starts off over the plain in search of Crusader.

He is not the only one at that moment making to find the horse. From the Indian camp a picked party has issued forth, urged by the chief. For the new leader of the Coyoteros longs to possess that now famous steed as much as did the deceased one.

"Ten of my best mustangs, and as many of my mules, will I give for the black horse of the pale-face. He who captures him may claim that reward."

More than once has El Zopilote thus de-
clared himself, exciting the ardour and cupidity
of his followers. Withal they have chased
Crusader in vain, over and over again, till in
their superstitious fancy they begin to think
him a phantom.

But as yet they have never tried to take him
by night; and now, having ascertained the
place where he usually passes the nocturnal
hours, they start out in quest of him.

Not rashly nor incautiously; instead, they
proceed deliberately, and with a preconceived
plan, as though stalking game. Their intention
is first to enfilade the animal at long distance
off, then contract the circle, so as to have him
sure.

In execution of their scheme, on reaching the
western side of the lake, they divide into two
parties. One moves along the mountain's foot,
dropping a file here and there; the other
strikes out over the *llano*, in a circular line, as
it proceeds doing the same.

It is too dark for them to see horse or other

object at any great distance, so they take care
that their circle be wide enough to embrace the
stretch of pasture where the coveted animal is
known to browse.

Noiselessly they execute the movement,
going at a slow walk, lest the hoof-strokes of
their horses may alarm the one they would
enclose; and when the heads of the separated
parties again come together, all know it by a
signal agreed upon—the cry of the coyote trans-
mitted along their line admonishes them that
the cordon is complete.

CHAPTER XXIV.

ONCE MORE UPON CRUSADER.

Henry Tresillian has hardly advanced a hundred yards from the cliff, when the Indian party, turning northward, passes close to the spot where he had been let down. Luckily not so close as to observe the rope still hanging there, and far enough from himself to hinder their seeing him. For the obscurity makes it impossible to distinguish objects unless very near.

Neither sees he them, nor has any suspicion of their dangerous proximity; and without stop or stay he keeps on towards the point where he expects to find his horse.

He goes not without a guide. At the latest hour of twilight he had seen Crusader about a mile off, in a direction due west; and although the night is dark, some of the stars are visible, among them the Polar. With this on his right shoulder he cannot mistake the way, so continues on in confidence.

He knows he will not need to go groping about, if the horse be still there, as it is hoped he is: a peculiarly intoned call with a whistle will bring him up from far as he can hear it. Many a time has his master, while hunting on the hills round Arispe, so summoned Crusader to his side.

He has advanced more than half a mile, and is thinking whether he shall not give the signal and put an end to all uncertainty. He should now be near enough for it to be heard, and it will tell him if the animal be still there or has wandered away to some other part of the *llano.* In the latter case all his labours will be lost, and no alternative left him but return to the cliff and get hoisted up again.

Still a thought holds him silent. The activity of the Indians, with their frequent patrol parties, more by night than by day, has long been a matter of curiosity and speculation among the miners. What if such a party be now out and within hearing? For he knows that to his voice Crusader will respond with a neigh, and that might undo all. Therefore, curbing his impatience, he proceeds on, silent as a spectre, his glances directed now this way, now that, endeavouring to penetrate the gloom.

All at once he hears the tramp of a horse, on the instant after seeing and recognizing Crusader. To his surprise also; for the animal is not at rest or browsing, but moving excitedly about, every now and then uttering a snort, as though he scented danger. His master knows he himself cannot be the cause of this unlooked-for behaviour. The horse is up wind, and could not possibly be aware of his approach. What, then, is exciting him?

Wolves—coyotes? Yes, it must be that; and as a proof of its being so, just then he hears the whining howl of the jackals simultaneously all around.

Such a chorus resounding on every side seems odd, the more from its being heard for but a brief moment, then silence as before. But Henry Tresillian stays not to reflect on its oddity. He fears that the howling repeated may start Crusader into a stampede, and without further delay gives him that signal he knows will be answered. Answered it is, and instantly, by a neigh sent back in response; and in twenty seconds after the horse stands face to face with his young master, his velvet muzzle pressing the latter's cheek. On one side there are words of endearment, on the other a low, joyous whimpering, as though the dumb brute was trying to speak its delight at their being together again.

Crusader opens his mouth to receive the bit, and seems almost to stoop for the saddle to be thrown over him. He is caparisoned in a trice; but just as Henry Tresillian, stooping to tighten the girths, gets the buckle into its hole, he hears that which causes him to rise erect, and clutch at the bridle: the sound of hoofs on all sides; horses evidently, with men upon their backs.   Indians!—they can be no other!

Quick as thought he vaults into the saddle, and sets himself ready to make a dash.

In what direction?   He knows that which he should take for Arispe.   But is it open to him?   This he cannot tell, nor, indeed, that any way is open to him.   For he now hears the tramp of horses all around, and before he can resolve himself, sees the horses themselves. It has grown a little clearer, for the moon is about to rise, and Crusader's neigh had guided the Indians to the spot.

If he stay, Henry Tresillian is conscious he will soon be encircled by a crowd with no chance to get clear of it.   Already he sees its ring closing around him.

But the Indians are still some fifty yards distant, come to a halt; suddenly and with shouts of surprise, for they have sighted him. There is even terror in their accents, with awe in their hearts—awe of the supernatural.   They supposed themselves making surround of a horse, when lo! there is a man upon his back, all in keeping with the mysterious character Crusader has obtained among those who have vainly chased him.

The young Englishman notes their strange behaviour, but without thought of the cause. He knows, however, they will not stay long at rest, and, by the better light, seeing a break in their line, sets his horse's head for it, gives the word with touch of knee, and springs forward at full speed, determined to take his chance.

In a dozen strides he is between two of the Coyotero horsemen, when he feels his bridle arm suddenly drawn back and held tight to his body; then, with a quick jerk he is lifted clean out of the saddle and flung with violence to the earth!

Fortunately he is neither stunned nor loses consciousness, but has all his senses about him; he knows what has happened, and that he is in the noose of a lasso. But his right arm is free, and, instantly regaining his feet, he draws his knife, and, severing the cord in twain, releases himself.

It would have been to little purpose had his horse been other than he is. But the sagacious animal, seeming to comprehend all, instead of galloping away, has stayed by his side, and in another moment has its master on its back again.

With to all appearance a clear track before him now, the daring youth once more makes forward, favoured by the confusion that has arisen among the savages. In the dim light they are unable to distinguish the strange horseman from one of themselves, and their surprise is but increased with their superstitious terror, both holding them spellbound. They but cry out, and question one another, without making any effort to pursue.

Henry Tresillian begins to think himself safe away, when he sees one of the Coyoteros, who had lagged behind their line, come full tilt towards him in a gallop as himself. Before he can check his pace, their animals meet in violent collision, and the mustang of the Indian is flung back on its haunches, dismounting its rider. The man has his gun in hand, and, seeing a pale-face, instinctively raises the piece, taking aim at him. But before he can touch the trigger, the English youth has also a piece levelled—a pistol, which cracks first; and the savage, uttering a wild agonized yell, staggers a pace or two, and falls backward on the grass.

With nothing more in his way now, his young master again gives Crusader the word, and off go they at highest race-course speed.

CHAPTER XXV.

IT is some time before the Indians recover from their mystification. Is the black horse flesh and blood, or a phantom?

Not until they have closed together and taken counsel of one another is this question resolved. The wiser of them affirm that in some way one of the pale-faces must have got down the cliff, caught the horse, and mounted him. That the rider, at least, is a mortal being they have ample evidence in their comrade stretched dead upon the plain by a bullet.

The sight rekindles all their ire, and shouts of vengeance make the welkin ring. But only for a while. Silence again reigns, and the hoof-strokes of the retreating fugitive can be

223

heard through the tranquil calm of the night, stirring them to pursuit.

Away go they in gallop after; but not all, nearly half of them turning their horses' heads towards the cliff. For if the white men have let one of their number down, there should be some sign of it, which they proceed to search for.

*   *   *   *   *

Impossible to depict the feelings of those on the *mesa*, above all, the ones who have been standing on the ledges to await the result. They cannot have themselves hoisted up again till sure their messenger has either failed or got free, and from the moment of his parting from the cliff's base, to them all had been uncertainty. Terrible suspense, too, from the very first; for although they saw not the Indians passing underneath, they heard their horses' tread, now and then a hoof striking against stone, or in dull thud upon the hard turf. Though they could not make out what it meant, they knew it was something adverse — hostile. Horses would not be there without men on their backs, and these must be enemies.

Listening on, with hearts anxiously beating, they hear that strange concatenation of cries, the supposed howling of coyotes, all around the plain. It puzzles them, too; but before they have time to reflect on it a sound better understandable reaches their ears—the neighing of a horse—most of them recognizing it as Crusader's, for most are familiar with its peculiar intonation.

More intently than ever do they listen now, but for a time hear nothing more. Only a brief interval; then arise sounds that excite their apprehension to its keenest—voices of men, in confused clamouring, the accent proclaiming them Indians.

Robert Tresillian, still standing beside the *gambusino* on the lowest ledge, feels his heart sink within him, as he exclaims:

" My poor boy! lost—lost!"

" Wait, señor," says Vicente, with an effort to appear calm. " That 's not so sure. All 's

not lost that's in danger. If there be a chance
of escape your brave son's the very one to take
advantage of it. *Oiga !* what's that ?"

His question has reference to another chorus
of cries heard out on the plain; then a moment's lull, succeeded by a crashing sound as
of two heavy bodies brought into collision.
After that a shot, quickly followed by a yell—
a groan.

"A pistol!" exclaims the *gambusino*, "and
sure the one Señorito Henrique took with him.
I'll warrant he's made good use of it."

The father is too full of anxious thought to
make reply; he but listens on with all ears, and
heart audibly pulsating.

Next to hear the hoof-strokes of a horse in
gallop as if going off; which in a way cheers
him : it may be his son escaped.

But then there is more confused clamour,
with loud ejaculations — voices raised in vengeance; and after the trampling of other horses,
apparently starting in pursuit.

What is to be done now?—draw up the rope,

and have themselves drawn up? There seems no reason for their waiting longer. The messenger is either safe off, or has been captured; one way or the other he will not get back there. So they may as well reascend the cliff.

Besides, a thought of their own safety now forces itself upon them. A streak of light along the horizon admonishes them of the uprising moon. Already her precursory rays, reflected over the plain, begin to lighten the obscurity, rendering objects more distinct, and they now make out a dark mass on the *llano* below, a party of horsemen, moving in the direction of the *mesa*.

"We'd better pull up, Don Roberto," says the *gambusino;* "they're coming this way, and if they see the rope it will guide their eyes to ourselves, and we're both lost men. They carry guns, and we'll be within easy range, not over thirty yards from them. *Por Dios!* if they sight us we're undone."

Don Roberto makes neither protest nor objection. By this his son has either got clear or is captured : in either case, he cannot return to them. And, as his companion, he is keenly sensible to the danger which is now threatening, so signifies assent. ·

Silently they draw up the rope, and soon as it is all in their hands, signal to those above to hoist them also. First one, making it fast round his body, is pulled up; then the loop is let down, and the other ascends, raised by an invisible power above.

Four are now on the next ledge, and, by like course of proceeding are lifted one after another to that still higher, the sloping benches between helping them in their ascent. All is done noislessly, cautiously; for the savages are now seen below in dark clump, stationary near the foot of the precipice.

They have reached the last bench, and so far unmolested, begin to think themselves out of danger,

But alas, no! The silence long prevailing is suddenly broken by a rock displaced and rolling down; while at the same moment the treacherous moon, showing over the horizon's edge, reveals them to the eyes of the Indians.

Then there is a chorus of wild yells, followed by shots—a very fusillade ; bullets strike the rocks and break fragments off, while other shots fired in return by those above into the black mass below instantly disperse it.

In the midst of all, the last man is drawn up to the summit, but when landed there, they who draw him up see that the rope's noose is no longer round a living body, but a corpse, bleeding, riddled with bullets.

CHAPTER XXVI.

FINDING himself clear of the Indians, Henry Tresillian's heart beats high with hope; no mischance happening, he can trust Crusader to keep him clear. And now he turns his thoughts to the direction he should take. But first to that in which he is going, for he has galloped out of the encircling line through the nearest opening that caught his eye.

The foretaste of the moonlight enables him to see where he is—luckily, on the right track. The route to Arispe lies south-eastward, and the lake must be passed at its upper or lower end. The former is the direct route, the other around about; but then there is the Indian camp to be got past, and others of the savages

230

may be up and about. Still the wagon *corral* is two or three hundred yards from the water's edge, which may give him a chance to pass between unobserved, and, with unlimited confidence in his horse, he resolves upon risking it.

An error of judgment : he has not taken into account the *fracas* behind, with the report of his own pistol, and that all this must have been heard by the red-skins remaining in camp. It has nevertheless. The consequence being that ere he has got half round the upper end of the lake, he sees the plain in front of him thickly dotted with dark forms—men on horseback—hears them shouting to one another. A glance shows him it is a gauntlet too dangerous to be run. The fleetness of his steed were no surety against gun-shots.

He reins up abruptly, and, with a wrench round, sets head west again, with the design to do what he should have done at first—turn the lake below.

The *détour* will be much greater now: he has passed a large elbow of it, which must be re-

passed to get around ; but there is no alternative, and, regretting his mistake, he makes along
the back track at best speed.   Not far before
finding further reason to be sorry for his blunder.
On that side, too, he sees mounted men directly
before him—those he had lately eluded.   They
are scattered all over the plain, apparently in
search of him, some riding towards the lake's
lower end, thinking he has gone that way.   But
all have their eyes on him now, and place themselves in position to intercept him.   His path is
beset on every side, the triumphant cries of the
Coyoteros proclaiming their confidence that they
have him at last—sure to capture or kill him
now.   And his own heart almost fails him : go
which way he will, it must be through a shower
of bullets.

Again he reins up, and sits in his saddle un-
decided.   The risk seems equal, but it must be
run ; there is no help for it.

Ha! yes, there is.   A thought has flashed
across his brain—a memory.   He remembers
having seen the camp animals wading the lake

through and through; not over belly-deep. Why cannot Crusader?

With quick resolve he sets his horse's head for the water, and in a second or two after the animal is up to the saddle-girths, plunging lightly as if it were but fetlock-deep.

Another cry from the Indians on both sides— surprise and disappointment mingled; in tones telling of their belief in the supernatural, and come back.

But soon they, too, recall the shallowness of the lake, and see nothing strange in the fugitive attempting to escape across it. So, without loss of time, they again put their horses to speed, making to head him on its eastern shore.

They are as near as can be to succeeding. A close shave it is for the pursued messenger, who, on emerging from the water, sees on either flank horsemen hastening towards him. But he is not dismayed. Before any of them are within shot range he dashes onward; Crusader, with sinews braced by the cool bath, showing speed which ensures him against being overtaken.

He is pursued, nevertheless. The subtle savages know there are chances and mischances. One of the latter may arise in their favour; and hoping it will be so, they continue the chase.

The moon is now up, everything on the level *llano* distinguishable for miles, and the black horse with his pale-faced rider is still less than twenty lengths ahead; so after him they go, fast as their mustangs can be forced.

Only to find that in brief time the twenty lengths have become doubled, then trebled, till in fine they see that it is fruitless to carry the pursuit further.

With hearts full of anger and chagrin, they give it up. Some apprehension have they as well. El Zopilote is not with them; what will he say on their returning empty-handed? what do? For it is now no mere matter of the catching of a horse; instead, more serious—a courier gone off to bring succour to the besieged.

Down-hearted and dejectedly they turn their horses' heads, and ride back for Nauchampa-tepetl.

*   *   *   *   *

Had the Coyoteros stuck to their faith in the probability of accidents and continued the pursuit, they might have overtaken Henry Tresillian after all. For scarce have they turned backs upon him when a mishap befalls him, not absolutely staying him in his course, but delaying him wellnigh an hour. He is making to regain the road which runs north from Arispe, at the point where the caravan, forced by want of water, had deflected from it to the Cerro Perdido. In daylight he could have ridden straight to it; for since then from the *mesa's* summit Pedro Vicente had pointed to guide-marks indicating the spot where his initials were carved upon the *palmida.* But in his haste now, amid the glamour of a newly-risen moon, the messenger has gone astray, only discovering it when his horse suddenly staggering forward comes down upon his knees, shooting him out of the saddle.

He is less hurt than surprised. Never before has Crusader made false step or stumble, and why now?

A moment reveals the reason: the ground has given way beneath, letting him down knee-deep into a hole, the burrow of some animal.

Fortunately, there are no bones broken, no damage done either to horse or rider; and the latter, recovering his seat in the saddle, essays to proceed. Soon to be a second time brought to a stand, though not now unhorsed. Crusader but lurches, keeping his legs, though again near going down.

The young Englishman perceives what it is: he is riding through a warren of the kind well known on the plains of Western America as "a prairie-dog town or village." In the moonlight he sees the hillocks of these marmots all around, with the animals themselves squatting on them; hears their tiny squirrel-like bark, intermingling with the hoot of the quaint little owl which shares their subterranean habitations.

Once more at halt, he again bethinks himself what is best to do. Shall he ride back and go round the village, or continue on across it, taking the chances of the treacherous ground?

He listens, soon to become assured that the pursuit has been abandoned, thus giving him choice to act deliberately, and do as seems best to him.

Around the dog town may be miles, while direct to the other side may be only a few score yards. They are often of oblong shape, extending far, but of little breadth, possibly because of the condition of the ground and the herbage it produces.

Having ridden into it, he resolves to keep on; but to his great annoyance and disgust finds it to extend far beyond the limits of his patience; and as Crusader's hoofs break through the hollow crust, it becomes necessary to alight and lead him.

At length, however, he is out of it, and again on firm ground, with the level *llano* far stretching before him. But in the distance he discerns a mountain ridge, trending north and south, lit up by the moon's light, along which, as he knows, lies the route to Arispe.

"We're on the right road now, my noble

Crusader, with no fear of being followed. And we must make it short as possible. The lives of many depend on that—on your speed, brave fellow. So let us on."

Crusader responds with one of his strangely-intoned whimperings—almost speech. Then stands motionless, till his young master is in the saddle; after which he again goes off in a gallop, *ventre a terre.*

CHAPTER XXVII.

IN PAINFUL SUSPENSE.

THAN the rest of that night no more anxious time has been spent by the beleaguered miners. If their new messenger fail in his errand, then they can never dispatch another. No chance for a second one to descend the cliff, or get down the gorge, for both will be hereafter guarded more carefully than ever.

All stay awake till morning, listening to every sound below, and doing what they can to interpret it. They had heard the cries near the Indian camp as Henry Tresillian attempted to pass it, those by the ravine's head hearing them plainer. Then other cries, as in response, proceeding from the western side of the lake.

After that a moment of silence, succeeded by a plunging noise, as of a horse making his way through deep water.   And soon after shouts again, for a while continuous, terminating in hoof-strokes, at each instant less distinct, at length dying away in the distance.

But just then they upon the cliff had to listen to other sounds more concerning themselves. For it was at this time their presence became known to the party remaining behind, resulting in that hurried ascent from ledge to ledge, with the loss of one of their number.

Long after, they see that which renews their excitement, their thoughts in a conflict between hope and fear.   From the vidette post, around which they have all gathered, they behold a moving mass, in the early dawn distinguishable as men on horseback,   It is the party who went in pursuit of their messenger returning.   But whether they have him with them or no cannot be told ; for they come back in a thick clump, and he may be in its midst invisible.   Nor is it opened out till they pass behind the abutment of rock, disappearing from the view of those on the *mesa.*

*　　　*　　　*　　　*　　　*

By the besieged ones the day is passed with anxiety unrelieved. For, although several had hastily proceeded to a point from which a sight of the Indian camp could be obtained, it was yet too dark to see whether the pursuers had brought back a prisoner. And when daylight came, he might be there without their being able to see him—inside the marquee, or under one of the wagons.

Gradually, however, their hopes gain the ascendant; for nothing of Crusader can be seen, and the noble steed, if there, could not well be hidden away. Besides, there is no more setting up of that ensanguined stake, no more firing at a human target, as would likely have taken . place had the pale-faced courier been their captive. Instead, a certain restlessness, with signs of apprehension, is observed among themselves throughout all the day, almost proclaiming his escape.

In Don Estevan's tent it is discussed, and this conclusion come to, giving joy to all. But to none as to his own daughter. All day a prey to keen, heart-sickening anxiety, how glad is she at hearing the *gambusino* say:

"I'm sure the señorito has got safe away, and is now on the road to Arispe. Were it not so, we'd have seen him ere this—tied to that accursed stake and riddled with bullets, as the others. The brutes meant doing the same with me; had almost begun it, when, thanks to the Virgin, there came a slip between cup and lip. And I think we may thank her now for giving a like chance to the brave lad. *Santos Dios!* he deserves it."

Cheering words to Gertrude, who can scarce resist rushing up to the speaker and giving him a kiss for them. Chaste kiss it would be, for the *gambusino* is neither young nor handsome. She contents herself by saying:

"Oh, sir! if he get safe to Arispe, you shall be paid for your saddle ten times over. I'm sure father will not grudge that."

"Saddle, *niña lindissima!*" exclaims Vicente, with a quizzical smile; "that's nought to me. I'd be glad to sacrifice a hundred such — ay, a thousand, if I could afford it, for him you seem so interested in. His life's too precious to be weighed in the scale against all the horsegear in the world."

All signify approval of these generous sentiments, so pleasing to the youth's father, who tacitly listens. And the brief dialogue over, they turn to discussing the chances of relief reaching them, now for the first time seeming favourable.

"If," says Don Estevan, hopeful as any, "he meet no accident before arriving at Arispe, then we may count on receiving succour. There's but one thing we have to fear—time! Nor need we fear that if Colonel Requenes be there with his regiment. By ill fortune he may not."

"What reason have you for thinking he may not?" asks Robert Tresillian.

"I recall his telling me, just before we started, that there was a likelihood of his being ordered to Guaymas, to assist in suppressing a reported rising of the Yaquis Indians. If he has gone thither we'll be no better off than before."

"But the people of Arispe—surely they will not be indifferent to our situation?"

It is the Englishman who interrogates.

"Ah, true," returns the Mexican, correcting himself, as a reassured expression comes over his countenance. "They will not. I did not think of that. I see it now."

"'T is not for us and ours alone we may expect them to bestir themselves; but for their own relatives and friends. Think, *amigo mio!* There isn't one of our following but has left some one behind who should rush to the rescue soon as hearing how things stand."

"You're right, Don Roberto. Whether the soldiers be there or not, Arispe and its surroundings can surely furnish force enough to effect our deliverance. We must have patience —hope and pray for it."

"Dear husband," here interposes the señora, "you seem to forget my brother, Juliano, and his three hundred *peones.* At least half of them are brave fellows, a match for any savages as these who surround us. If Henrique succeed in reaching Arispe, he will go on to my brother's *hacienda*, soldiers or no soldiers."

This speech from an unexpected quarter further heightens their hopes, already rapidly rising. They almost feel as if the siege was being raised, and themselves about to continue their long-delayed journey.

A like sentiment pervades the people all through the camp. In every shed and booth is a group conversing on the same topic, and much in a similar way; all with trusting reliance on the friends left behind, confident they will not fail them.

* * * * *

At this self-same hour the feeling in the Coyotero camp is quite the contrary: instead of confidence, there is doubt, even apprehension. The white men's messenger—for they are sure he must have been this—has got through their lines, clear away, and well do they comprehend the consequences.

They know the miners come from Arispe—marks on the wagons and other chattels tell them that—and the pale-face courier will be now hastening thither. On such a swift steed he will reach it in quick time; and, with the tale which he has to tell, alike quick will be the response: a rescuing host in rush for Nauchampa-tepetl. It may even arrive before the return of their raiders from the Horcasitas.

Thus apprehensive, on the day and night following the escape of Henry Tresillian, and for many days and nights after, there is as much, if not more, anxiety in the camp of the besiegers as in that of the besieged.

The latter fear but famine; the former, fire and sword.

CHAPTER XXVIII.

FRIENDS IN FEAR.

"GLAD to see you, Señor Juliano! It's not often you honour Arispe with your presence."

Colonel Requenes is the speaker, he spoken to being a gentleman of middle age, in civilian costume, the dress of a *haciendado*. It is Don Juliano Romero, brother of the Señora Villanueva, the owner of a large *ganadería* or grazing estate, some six or seven miles out of Arispe.

"True," he admits, "nor would you see me now, only that this thing begins to look serious."

"What thing?" asks the Colonel, half divining it.

"No news from Villanueva. I came to see if *you've* had any."

247

"Not a word; and you're right about it's beginning to look serious. I was just talking of it to your son there, before you came in."

They are in a large apartment in Colonel Requenes' official residence, his receiving-room, into which the *ganadero* has just been ushered; the son alluded to being there already, a youth of some sixteen summers, in military uniform, with sabretasche and other insignia proclaiming him an aide-de-camp. After greeting his father, he has resumed his seat by a table on which are several open despatches, with which he seems to busy himself.

"*Por Dios!* I cannot tell what to make of it," pursues the *ganadero;* "they must have reached the mine, wherever it is, long ago. Time enough for word to have been brought back. And my sister not writing to me, that's a puzzle! She promised she would soon as they got there."

"And Villanueva himself promised he would write to me. Besides, the people, many of them, have left friends behind, relatives out in the neigbourhood of the old *minera*. Some of them are in Arispe every day, inquiring if there be any news of those gone north; so it's clear they've had no word from them either."

"What do you suppose can be the cause, Requenes?"

"I've been trying to think. At first I fancied the great drought that's been, with every stream and pond dried up, might have forced them out of their way for water, and so lengthened their journey. But even with that there's been time enough for them to have reached their destination long since, and us to have heard of it. As we haven't, I fear it's something worse."

"What's your conjecture, Colonel?"

"I'm almost afraid to venture on conjectures, but they force themselves on me, Don Juliano; and in the one shape you will yourself, no doubt, be thinking of."

"I comprehend. *Los Indios!*"

"*Los Indios,*" echoes the officer; "just that. Villanueva told me the new-discovered *veta* lies a long way to the north-west, beyond the head-waters of the Horcasitas. That's all country claimed by the Apaches of different bands; as you know, every one of them determinedly hostile to the whites, especially to us Mexicans, for reasons you may have heard of."

"I know all that; you allude to the affair of Gil Perez?"

"I do; and my fear is our friends may have encountered these red-handed savages. If so, Heaven have mercy on them, and God help them; for He only can."

"Encountering them would mean being attacked by them?"

"Surely so; and destroyed if defeated: the men butchered, the women and children carried into captivity."

At this the young aide-de-camp turns round on his chair, his face showing an expression of pain. He says nothing, however, but continues an earnest listener to the conversation.

"Merciful Heaven!" exclaims the *ganadero*, with a groan, "I hope it has not come to that."

"I hope so too, and don't yet think it has; only that it's probable enough—too probable. Still, even if set upon, they would resist; and when one comes to remember how many there were of them, they ought to make a stout resistance."

"Many of them," rejoins Don Juliano, "both miners and *vaqueros*, are of approved valour, and were well armed. I was at the old *minera* when they started off, and saw that for myself."

"Yes, I know; but their holding out would depend on the sort of ground they chanced to be on when attacked, if they have been attacked. By good luck, our mutual brother-in-law is no novice to Indian tactics, but a soldier of experience, who'll know how to act in any emergency."

"True; but the worst of it is his being embarrassed by having so many women and children with him; among them, alas! my sister and niece. *Pobrecitas!*"

Again the young officer shifts uneasily on his chair, the expression of pain still upon his face.

For he is the cousin whom Gertrude was said to have forgotten.

"They took a number of large vehicles with them?" says the Colonel, interrogatively. "American wagons, did they not?"

"They did."

"How many? Can you remember?"

"Six or seven, I think."

"And a large pack-train?"

"Yes; the *atajo* seemed to number about fourscore mules."

For a moment the Colonel is silent, seeming to reflect, then says:

"Villanueva would know how to throw these *carros* into *corral*, and with so many pack-saddles ought to make a defencible breastwork, to say nothing of the bales and boxes of goods. If not taken by surprise while *en route*, he'd be sure of using that precaution. So protected, and armed as they were, they ought to hold good their ground against any number of red-skins. The worst danger would be their getting dropped on in some place without water.

In that case surrender would be the necessary result, and surrender to Apaches were as death itself."

"*Santissima!* yes—we all know that. But, Requenes, do you really think we've to fear their having met such a disaster?"

"I don't know what to think. I'd fain not fear it, but the thing looks grave, no matter in what way one views it. There should have been word from them several days ago; none coming, what other can be the explanation?"

"Ay, true; what other?" rejoins the *ganadero*, despondently. "But what ought we to do?" he adds.

"I've been considering that for some time, but couldn't make up my mind. I've made it up now."

"To what?"

"To sending one of my squadrons along the route they took; with orders to follow it up, if need be, to the new-discovered mine; at all events, till it be ascertained what hinders our hearing from them."

"That seems the best and only way," returns Don Juliano. "But when do you propose your men to start?"

"Immediately—soon as they can be ready. For such an expedition, most of the way through a very wilderness, they will need supplies, however lightly equipped. But I will issue the order this moment. Cecilio," to the aide-de-camp, "hasten down to the *cuartel*, and tell Major Garcia to come to me at once."

The young officer, rising at the words and clapping on his shako, makes straight for the outer door. But before stepping over its threshold, he sees that which causes him to return instantly to the receiving-room, to the surprise of those he had left there.

"What is it?" demands the Colonel.

"Look there!"

He points out through the open window over the *plaza* in front of it. Springing from their seats and moving up to it, they perceive a young man on horseback advancing towards the house; his face pale, and with a wayworn

THE DEAD POSTILION.—p 253

look, his dress dust-stained, and otherwise out of order, the horse he bestrides steaming at the nostrils, froth · clouted, and with palpitating flanks.

"*Caramba!*" exclaims Colonel Requenes. "That's young Tresillian, the son of Villanuevas' partner!".

CHAPTER XXIX.

TO THE RESCUE.

IN an instant after Henry Tresillian is inside the room, warmly received by both the Colonel and *ganadero;* less so by the young officer, though the two had been formerly bosom friends. The coolness of Cecilio Romero can be easily understood; but in the scene which succeeds, with hasty questioning, and answers alike hurried, no one takes note of it.

"You bring news—bad news, I fear?" says the Colonel.

"Bad, yes. I'm sorry having to say so," returns the messenger. "This is for you, señor —from Don Estevan Villanueva. 'T will tell you all."

He pulls a folded paper from under his jacket, and hands it to the Colonel.

Breaking it open, the latter reads aloud; Romero standing by and listening, for its contents concern them all.

Thus ran it :

"*Hermano mio* (brother),--

"If Heaven permit this to reach your hands, 't will tell you how we are situated—in extreme peril, I grieve to say, surrounded by Apache Indians, the most hostile and cruel of all—the Coyoteros. Where and how I need not specify. The brave boy who bears this, if successful in putting it into your hands, will give you all details. When you've got them, I know how you will act, and that no appeal from me is necessary. On you alone depends our safety —our lives. Without your help we are lost.

"ESTEVAN VILLANUEVA."

"They shall not be lost," cries the Colonel, greatly agitated—"not one of them, if the Zacatecas Lancers can save them. I go to their aid; will start at once. Away, Cecilio! down

to the *cuartel!* Bring Major Garcia back with
you immediately. Now, señorito," he adds,
turning to Henry Tresillian, "the details. Tell
us all. But, first, where are our friends in such
peril? In what place are they surrounded?"

"In a place strange enough, Señor Colonel,"
answers the young Englishman. "On the top
of a mountain."

"On the top of a mountain!" echoes the
Colonel. "A strange situation, indeed. What
sort of mountain?"

"One standing alone on the *llanos*, out of
sight of any other. 'T is known as the Cerro
Perdido."

"Ah! I've heard of it."

"I too," says the *ganadero*.

"Up somewhere near the sources of the
Horcasitas. A singular eminence—a *mesa*, I
believe. But how came they to go there?
It must be some way off the route to their
intended destination."

"We were forced thither, señor, through
want of water. The guide advised it, and his

advice would have been for the best, but for
the ill luck of the savages chancing to come
along that way."

"*Muchacho*, I won't confuse you with further
questioning, but leave you to tell your tale.
We listen.   First have a *copita* of Catalan
brandy to refresh you.   You seem in need of
it."

"There's one needs refreshing as much as
myself, Señor Colonel; ay, more, and more
deserves it."

"What one!   Who?"

"My horse out there.   But for him I would
not be here."

"Ah! that's your grand steed," says the
Colonel, looking out; "I remember him—Crusader.   He does seem to need it, and shall
have it. *Sargento!*"   This in loud call to an
orderly sergeant in waiting outside, who, instantly showing his face at the door, receives
command to see the black horse attended to.

"Now, *muchacho mio!* proceed."

Henry Tresillian, still speaking hurriedly for

reasons comprehensible, runs over all that has occurred to the caravan, since its departure from the worked-out mine near Arispe, till its arrival at the Lost Mountain. Then the unexpected approach of the Indians, resulting in the retreat to the summit of the Cerro, with the other incidents and events succeeding—to that, the latest, of himself being lowered down the cliff, and his after-escape through the fleetness of his matchless steed.

"How many of the Indians are there?" asks the Colonel. "Can you tell that, señorito?"

"Between four and five hundred, we supposed; but they were not all there when I left. Some days before half their number went off on a marauding expedition southward; so our guide believed, as they were dressed and painted as when on the war-trail."

"These had not returned when you came away?"

"No, Señor Colonel; no sign of them."

"I see it all now, and pity the poor people who live on the lower Horcasitas. That's where they were bent for, no doubt. The more reason for our making haste to reach the Cerro Perdido. We may catch these raiders on return. *Sarjento!*" This again in call to the orderly, who responds instantly by presenting himself in the doorway.

"Summon the bugler! Give him orders to sound the 'assembly' at once. We must start without a moment's delay. How fortunate those Yaquis kept quiet, else I would be now operating around Guaymas."

"We must, Requeñes. But will your regiment be enough? How many men can you muster?"

"Five hundred. But there's the battery of moutain howitzers—fifty men more. Of course, I take that along."

"And of course I go too," says the *ganadero;* "and, to make sure of our having force sufficient, can take with me at least a hundred good men, the pick of my *vaqueros.* Fortunately they're now all within easy summons, assembled at my house for the *herradero*" (cattle branding), "which was to come off to-morrow. That can be postponed. *Hasta luego,* Colonel; I ride back home to bring them; so doubt not my having them here, and ready for the route soon as your soldiers.

"*Bueno!* Whether needed or not, it will be well to have your valiant *vaqueros* with us. I'll welcome them."

Instantly after the *plaza* of Arispe displays an animated scene, people crowding into it from all parts, with air excited. For the report, brought by the young Englishman, has gone forth and all abroad, spreading like wildfire,— Villanueva and Tresillian, with all their people, surrounded by savages! "*Los Indios!*" is the cry carried from point to point, striking terror into the hearts of the Arispeños, as though the dreaded red-skins, instead of being at an un- known distance off, were at the gates of their city.

Then succeeds loud cheering as the bugle- call proclaims the approach of the *lanzeros,* troop after troop filing into the *plaza,* and forming line in front of their colonel's quarters, all in complete equipment, and ready for the route.

More cheering as Don Juliano Romero comes riding in at the head of his hundred retainers; *vaqueros* and *rancheros*, in the picturesque costume of the country, armed to the teeth, and mounted on their mustangs, fresh, fiery, and prancing.

Still another cheer, as the battery of mountain howitzers rolls in and takes its place in the line. Then a loud chorus of *vivas!* as the march commences, prolonged and carried on as the column moves through the street; the crowd following far beyond the suburbs, to take leave of it with prayers upon their lips for the successful issue of an expedition in which many of them are but too painfully interested.

CHAPTER XXX.

THE RAIDERS RETURNED.

ANOTHER ten days have elapsed, and they on the Cerro Perdido are held there rigorously as ever ; a strong guard kept constantly stationed at both points where it is possible for them to reach the plain.

In the interval no incident of any note has arisen to vary the monotony of their lives. One day is just as the other, with little to occupy them, save the watch by the ravine's head, which needs to be maintained with vigilance unabated.

But much change has arisen both in their circumstances and appearance. With provision wellnigh out, they have been for days on less than half allowance, and famine has set its stamp on their features. Pallid, hollow cheeks, with eyes sunken in their sockets, are seen all around; and some of the weaker ones begin to totter in their steps, till the place more resembles the grounds of an hospital than an encampment of travellers. They have miscalculated their resources, which gave out sooner than expected.

In this lamentably forlorn condition they are still uncertain as to the fate of their messenger, their doubts about his safety increasing every day—every hour. Not that they suppose him to have fallen into the hands of the Coyoteros. On the contrary, they are convinced of his having escaped, else some signs of his capture would have been apparent in the Indian camp, and none such are observed. But other contingencies may have arisen: an accident to himself, or his horse, delaying him on the route, if not stopping him altogether.

Or may it be, as Don Estevan has said, that Colonel Requeñes with his soldiers is absent from Arispe, and there is a difficulty in raising a force of civilians sufficient for effecting their rescue ?

These conjectures, with many others, pass through their minds, producing a despondency, now at its darkest and deepest. For at first, in their impatience, blind to probabilities, they fancied theirs a winged messenger—a Mercury, who should have brought them succour long since. That bright dream is passed, and the reaction has set in, gloomy as shadow of death itself.

Nor seems there to be much cheer in the camp of their besiegers. They can look down upon it from a distance near enough to distinguish the individual forms of the savages, and note all their actions in the open. Through the telescope can be read even the expressions on their features, showing that they, too, have their anxieties and apprehensions; no doubt from the black horse and his rider having got away from them.

Their scouts are still observed to come and go. Some are sent northward, others to the south ; the last evidently to look out for the return of the raiding party gone down the Horcasitas.

Another day passes, and they are seen coming back, at a pace which betokens their bringing a report of an important nature. That it is a welcome one to their comrades in the camp can be told by their shouts of triumph as they approach.

Soon after they upon the *mesa* are made aware of the cause, by seeing the red marauders themselves coming on towards the camp, in array very different from that when leaving it. Instead of only their arms and light equipments, every man of them is now laden with spoil, every horse besides his rider carrying a load, either on withers or croup. And they have other horses with them now—a *caballada* —mules, too, all under pack and burden.

No, not all. As the long straggling line draws closer to the Cerro, they on its summit see a number of these animals bearing on their backs something more than the loot of plun-

dered houses. They see women, most of them
appearing to be young girls.

·As they are conducted on to the camp, and
inside its enclosure, Don Estevan, viewing them
through his telescope, can trace upon their
persons, as their features, all the signs and
lines proclaiming utter despair : dresses torn,
hair hanging dishevelled, and eyes downcast,
with not a ray or spark of hope in them.

Others look through the glass, to be pained
by the heart-saddening spectacle ; each of the
married ones, as he views it, thinking of his
own wife or daughter, in fear their fate may be
the same—a fate too horrid to be dwelt upon
in thought, much less to be talked about.

This day they are not permitted to see more.
Twilight is already on, and night's darkness,
almost instantly succeeding, shuts out from
their view everything below.

But if they see not, they can hear. There
are continuous noises in the camp throughout
the rest of the night—cries and joyous ejaculations. The Coyoteros have made a grand *coup:*

much plunder acquired, many prisoners taken, and pale-faced foes slain, almost to a glut of vengeance. They are greatly jubilant, and yield themselves to a very pæan of rejoicing, their boasts and exulting shouts at intervals reverberating along the cliffs.

It is another night of carousal with them, as that when they first sate down to the siege ; for among the proceeds of their recent maraud are several pig-skins of *aguardiente*, and this fiery spirit, freely distributed, excites them almost to madness.

So loud are their yells, so angrily, vengefully intoned, that they who listen above begin to fear they may at length become reckless, and, *coûte que coûte*, risk the assault so long un-attempted. In such numbers now, feeling their strength, they may hold a little loss light. Be-sides, there is still that apprehension from the side of Arispe ; it may further urge them to a desperate deed, which, if not done at once, must be left undone, and the siege ingloriously abandoned.

These are but the conjectures of the besieged, who, acting upon them, keep watch throughout the remainder of the night. Never more wakeful, seemingly, though never less needed; for up till the hour of dawn, no assailant is seen approaching the gorge, no sound heard of any one attempting to scale that steep acclivity.

Of those fearing that they will try, Pedro Vicente is not among the number. Endeavouring to give confidence to his doubting companions, he says,

" I know the Coyoteros too well to suppose them such fools. Not all the *aguardiente* in Sonora will make them mad enough to expose themselves to our battery of stones. They don't forget our having it here, and that we 're watching their every movement; ready to rain a storm of rocks on them if they but come under its range. So, *camarados,* keep up heart and courage! We 've nothing more to fear to-day than we had yesterday. That's hunger, not their spears or scalping-knives."

Fortified by the *gambusino's* words, they to

whom they are addressed feel their confidence restored—enough to inspire them with further patience and endurance.

CHAPTER XXXI.

"Soh! that's the Lost Mountain, is it?"

"It is, Colonel."

"*Gracias a Dios!* Glad we've sighted it at last. How far do you think we're from it, señorito? Nigh twenty miles, I take it; though it looks nearer."

"'T is all of twenty miles, Colonel; so our guide said when we first saw it from the place."

"I can quite believe it. On these high plains distances are very deceptive; but my experience enables me to judge pretty correctly."

The dialogue is between Colonel Requeñes and Henry Tresillian; the latter acting as guide to the expedition *en route* to release those imprisoned on the Cerro Perdido. Others are

272

beside them; Don Juliano with his son, the young aide-de-camp, and several officers of the staff; their escort forming an advanced guard. Not far behind it, the howitzer battery, followed by the lancer regiment in open order; then Romero's irregulars, closed by a troop of lancers as rear-guard, completing the marching column.

All are at halt, brought to it as soon as the Cerro was sighted. They have been on march from an early hour by moonlight, and as the sun, now rising, has lit up the plain afar, the solitary eminence can be clearly seen. As may be deduced from the young Englishman's words, the point they have arrived at is the same where the caravan had temporarily come to a stop— the very spot itself; for close by is the tree bearing the initials of the *gambusino.*

"Well, *caballeros,*" continues the Colonel, "we've done our best so far; pray God to good purpose. Let us hope we're in time. I wonder how it is? What's your thought, Romero?

"I have none, Requeñes—only hopes that they've held out."

"I wish," pursues the Colonel, in half soliloquy, "we but knew for certain; 't would make an important difference as to how I dispose of my force. Should they be still there——"

"Señor Colonel," interposes the youthful guide, "if you'll let me have a look through your telescope, I think I can settle that point."

This, as he sees the commanding officer drawing his field-glass from its case.

"In welcome, señorito. Here!" and he hands him the telescope.

Instantly it is brought to his eye, and eagerly —his fingers trembling as they hold it out. What he hopes to see will tell him that his father and friends still live; if he sees it not, he will know they are dead; and *she*, dearer than all, condemned to a fate far worse!

What a change comes over his countenance almost on the instant of his raising the glass to his eye! Hitherto grave to apprehension, all at once it lights joyously up, as from his lips proceed the words,

" They're still on the mountain ; Heaven be praised !"

" If it be so, Heaven deserves praise—all our thanks. But how know you, señorito ? "

" By the flag !"

" What flag ? "

" Take the glass, Colonel; look for yourself."

Receiving back the telescope, and adjusting it to his sight, Requeñes levels it at the Lost Mountain.

"At the nearest end, up on the summit," pursues Henry Tresillian, instructingly, " you'll see it. It is the flag of Mexico. Don Estevan intended to have raised it over his new mine, and had it hoisted yonder in the hope it might be seen by some white men, and lead to our situation being made known. It has proved of service now ; telling us our friends are still in the land of the living. If they were not it wouldn't be there."

" You're right, señorito, it wouldn't. And it is there—I see it !—yes, can even make out the national insignia — the eagle and nopal. We may thank Heaven, indeed."

" And we do ! " exclaims the *ganadero*, raising his hat reverentially, all following his example.

A thrill of exultation runs like wildfire backward on to the extremest rear—a joyous excitement, as the soldiers learn they have not made their long march in vain, and that the foe is before them, not far off. For the banner waving above proclaims the siege still continued, and the Indians keeping it up.

" They *are* there," affirms the Colonel, after gazing some time through his glass. " I can see the smoke ascending from their camp fires. No doubt by this they'll be cooking their breakfasts. Well, we won't be in time to hinder their having that meal ; but if they eat dinner this day, without my leave, I shall be willing to throw up my commission as colonel of the Zacatecas Lancers. Now, gentlemen ! " he adds, turning to his staff, and summoning his chief officers around him in council of war, "the enemy is yonder ; no doubt of it. 'T is a

THE RESCUERS.—p. 27

question as to how we should advance upon him. Give your opinion, Major Garcia."

"How many are there supposed to be, Colonel?" asks the major, a sage, grizzled veteran. "Our mode of approaching them should much depend upon that."

"Unluckily I can't tell," says the Commander-in-chief; "there were wellnigh five hundred all told when together; but it appears that half went off on a raid down the Horcasitas, the other half remaining to carry on the siege. If the raiders are returned and are now among the besiegers, then we'll have their full force to deal with, and may expect a sharp fight for it. I know these red-skins of old, the band of the Rattlesnake; though, as our young friend informs me, that worthy has ceased to exist, and the Vulture reigns in his stead. All the worse for us, as Zopilote was the master of Cascabel in tactics, cunning, courage—everything. Never mind, we should only be too glad to meet the renowned warrior, if but for glory's sake."

While the Colonel is still speaking a voice is

heard to rearward, with exclamations telling of
excitement there. Immediately after a subal-
tern officer of the rear-guard advances rapidly
to the front, conducting a strange horseman,
whose dress, travel-stained, with the sweat and
dust upon his horse, betokens him just arrived
from a journey long and hurriedly made. A
messenger on some errand, which his wan, woe-
begone face bespeaks to be of the saddest.

"Whence come you, *amigo?*" demands the
commanding officer, as the stranger is brought
face to face with him.

"From Nacomori, on the Horcasitas, Señor
Colonel," is the answer.

"On what business?" asks Requeñes, more
than half divining it.

"Oh, señor, the Indians have been there;
killed scores of our people—children as grown
men; plundered and burnt our houses; carried
off all our young women; made rack and ruin
of everything. I rode to Arispe, hoping to find
you there, but you were gone, and I've has-
tened hither after you."

"What Indians? Where did they come from?"

"From the north, señor; down the river. Apaches, we thought; but it was in the night they came upon us, and no one could be sure. When morning came they had gone off with everything."

"What night? How long since this occurred?"

"The night of *Lunes*—just four days ago."

"The raiding party of the Coyoteros, gentlemen," says the Colonel to his surrounding. "The time corresponds, the place—everything; and likely they've got back, and are now by the Cerro yonder. If so, we have others to rescue beside our own friends; with chastisement to 'nflict on the red-handed marauders, to say nothing of revenge. So much the more reason for our not losing time. Major! order the regiment to close up and form line. Let the others be drawn in also; I want to say a word to them."

With a quickness due to thorough discipline,

the lancers are brought into battle line; not for
fight now, but to receive an address. Thrown
forward on one flank, and facing inwards, are
the light artillerists; while on the other in file
form are Romero's irregulars.

Placing himself in a position to be heard by
all, the Commander-in-chief cries out :

"*Camarados!* at the base of yonder hill,
where you see smoke rising, is the enemy.
Apaches—Coyoteros—as we know, knowing
them also to be the cruellest of all the savages
that infest our frontier. To say nothing of the
glory gained in conquering them, 't will be
doing humanity a service to destroy them ; and
never more than now has there been reason.

" This gentleman "—he points to the newly-
arrived messenger, still on horseback and near
by—" has brought news of a bloodthirsty massacre they have just committed at Nacomori,
on the Horcasitas, where women, scores, have
been carried off. Like enough they're all over
yonder now, and we may be in time to release
these prisoners, and avenge the murders that

have been done. The only fear is of the Indians getting away from us. Mounted on their swift mustangs, and leaving all encumbrances behind, that is still possible enough. But to prevent it, I intend dividing my force, and sending detachments around to intercept and cut off their retreat on every route they may take. We must deal them a death-blow, and I now call on you—every man to do his best. Remember how many of our people, perhaps many of your own relatives, have fallen victims to the ferocity of these ruthless marauders. Think of the crime we have just heard of at Nacomori. Think of it, *camarados,* and strike home!"

An enthusiastic cheer hails the Colonel's speech; and while it is still ringing commands are issued for the disposition of the advance—the movement soon after commencing.

CHAPTER XXXII.

Not an hour of daylight now passes, scarce a minute, without Don Estevan Villanueva or Robert Tresillian having the telescope to their eyes, scanning the plain southward. For days this has been their practice, up to that on which the red marauders are seen returning from their murderous expedition.

And on the following morning at earliest dawn the two—Pedro Vicente along with them —take their stand on an outward projection of the *mesa*, which commands a view of the *llano* all round its southern side, at the same time overlooking the Coyotero camp.

They have not been long there when, under the first rays of the rising sun, they see something sparkle which had never been observed by them before, though in a place with which they are familiar—the same where they first sighted the Cerro Perdido. Nor is the glancing object a single one, for there are many shining points as stars in a constellation. They are visible to the naked eye, for as yet none of them have looked through the telescope. As Don Estevan is levelling it, the *gambusino* says:

"Looks like the glitter of arms and accoutrements. Pray the Virgin it be that!"

"It *is* that!" cries Don Estevan, at the first glance through the glass. "Arms, and in the hands of men. I can make out a body of horse in uniform—soldiers. Requeñes and his regiment; he to a certainty. At length—at last—we may hope to be rescued, and our long imprisonment brought to an end."

His words, spoken excitedly and aloud, attract those who are sauntering near, and soon most upon the *mesa* come clustering round him. To see with eyes unaided that metallic sheen, as they eagerly hearken to its interpretation. Don Estevan, with the telescope still held aloft, goes on speaking :

" Yes ; 't is they ! I can see they carry lances, by the sun glinting on the blades above their heads. They can be no other than the Zacatecas regiment, with my brother-in-law at its head. Your son, Tresillian, is safe ; their being yonder tells of his having reached Arispe. Brave youth ! we all owe him our blessing."

" And we give him that, with our gratitude !" shouts Pedro Vicente, the others enthusiastically echoing his words.

There is a momentary lull, all ears intently listening for what Don Estevan may next say ; which is :

" They appear to be extending line, and look as if there were a good six or seven hundred. Ah ! now I note there are others besides the lancers—a battery of brass guns—that's what's flashing back the sun. And a body of horsemen, not in uniform. They seem to be at halt. Why and for what ?"

"Like enough," suggests Tresillian, "they've made out our flag telling them we are still here. Requeñes, with others of his officers, will have telescopes too, and must see it, as also that smoke over the camp below. It will tell them our besiegers are there also. That would cause them to halt—to concert measures for the attack."

"You're right, Don Roberto, it must be as you say. But now there's a movement among them. The mass is breaking up into detachments, some commencing to march to the right, others to the left. Ah! I see it all : they mean making a surround, cutting off the retreat of our enemy. *Caramba !* Requeñes *is* a cunning strategist, as I always believed him."

With the glass still at his eye, the old soldier can see every movement made, comprehending all, and explaining them in succession to the audience around him. A party of lancers, seemingly a squadron, separating from the main body, moves off to the right, another party of like strength proceeding in the opposite direction. Then other detachments follow these, as if to form an enfilading line when the time comes for it. But the central force remains stationary long after the flanking parties have been extended, and is only seen to advance when they are far away. These make wide circuit, evidently designed to embrace the Coyoteros' camp, and, if need be, the Cerro itself.

And now they draw nearer till all upon the *mesa*, without any artificial aid, can see they are men, and as such surely friends hastening to their rescue.

To their joy they also perceive that the occupants of the Indian camp are as yet unaware of what is approaching. Five hundred feet below, their view is more limited; and long before the soldiers become visible to them, they above see the latter distinctly, and understand their strategic scheme.

Meanwhile the savages are not acting in the ordinary way: signs of commotion are observable among them, as if some change were intended. Horses are being caught and caparisoned, while the newly acquired animals from the Horcasitas are again loaded with the spoils, those that carried the captives being also made ready for the road.

The women are themselves seen within the *corral;* as on the evening before, looking forlorn, every one of them a picture of despair. They are to be taken they know not whither, but to a place from which they have no hope of return. Little dream they that friends are so near.

"What a pity we can't let them know of rescue being at hand!" says Don Estevan. "They could hear us if we call to them, but some of the Coyoteros are acquainted with our language, and it would warn them also."

"No fear of that," affirms the *gambusino;* "I think I can speak a tongue that the redskins won't understand, and the women will."

"What tongue?" asks Don Estevan.

"The Opata. Some of those girls are *mestizas,* and should know the lingo of their mothers."

"Try them with it, then, Don Pedro."

"With your worship's leave, I will."

Saying which, the *gambusino* advances to the outermost edge of the cliff, and, with all the strength of his lungs, utters some words altogether unintelligible to those around him, but evidently understood by the captives below.

Several of them on hearing it spring suddenly to their feet, looking up in the direction whence it came, surprised to see men above, hitherto unobserved by them, and still more to hear speech addressed to themselves. Hope and joy become mingled with their astonishment, when the *gambusino* goes on in the same vernacular to tell them how it is, and that succour is near.

Though listening all the while, not one of the Apaches appears to comprehend a word of what Vicente is saying. They suppose it a mere expression of sympathy; and, without giving heed to it, proceed with their preparations for departure. They are evidently bent upon this, though it may be but the raiders about to continue on to their home in Apacheria. Still, other signs seem to indicate a general clearing out of the camp; for now the whole *caballada* of horses are being brought in saddled and bridled, while everything portable in the way of goods is turned out within the *corral*, packed as if for transportation.

And in reality it is their intention to abandon both camp and siege, though reluctantly, and hating to surrender a chance of revenge that had seemed so sure and near. But they have had enough to content them for the time, and there is a fear which forces them to forego it. Ever since Henry Tresillian escaped them they have been nervously apprehensive, correctly surmising him a messenger. He must long since have reached Arispe, and may at any moment reappear, guiding back a force sufficient to overwhelm them.

While yet unrecovered from their night's carousal, it is as the fulfilment of a dream, their worst apprehensions realized, as they behold coming towards them, though still far off, a

19

body of men, uniformed and in serried array, with pennoned lances borne aloft!

The sight is not so much a surprise, neither does it produce a panic ; for they who approach seem not in such numbers as to overawe them. The detached parties sent around are not within their view, and with their habitual contempt for the Mexican *soldados*, they make light of those that are, imagining them under a mistake — advancing upon an enemy whose strength they have underrated.

The error is their own ; but, misled by it, they resolve to ride out, meet the pale-faced foemen, and anticipate their attack. Their chief so commands it.

Quick as thought every warrior is upon his horse, gun or spear in hand ; they, too, in military formation—line of battle—pressing forward to the encounter, the sentries alone left on post.

CHAPTER XXXIII.

THE THUNDER GUNS.

As is their custom, the savages advance with loud cries and gestures of menace, intended to terrify their antagonists.

They have got several miles out from the mountain, and almost within charging distance, when they see that which brings them to sudden halt—a thing above all others dreaded by the American aboriginal—cannon "thunder guns" —as they call them. The brass howitzers, hitherto screened by the vanguard of cavalry, have been thrown to the front, instantly unlimbered, and so brought under their eyes. Then a flash, a vomiting of flame and smoke, a loud ringing report, followed by the hurtling of a shell in its flight through the air. It drops in their midst and instantly explodes, its severed fragments dealing death around.

Too much this for Coyotero courage; and without waiting for other like destructive missiles to follow, they turn tail and gallop back towards the camp. Not that they have any hope of safety there, for they believe the great thunder guns can reach them anywhere, and their flight towards it is but the impulse of a confused fear.

The sentries, seeing them in retreat, alike frightened by the report of the howitzers, forsake their posts, each hastening towards a horse—his own.

For a time the captive women are unguarded, seemingly forgotten. It gives the *gambusino* a cue; and, acting upon it, he again calls out as before in the Opata tongue,

"Sisters! now's your time! Up and out of the *corral;* make round to the lake, fast as you can run, and on into the ravine. There you'll find friends to meet you."

Listening to his counsel, as one the captive

women resolve to act upon it; for they are now cognizant of what is going on, and fully comprehend the situation.

The result, a rush out of the enclosure all together, and a race round to the spot indicated by that friendly voice above.

They reach it, to find there the man himself, with over twoscore others around him. For the *gambusino*, seeing how things stood, and that the besiegers had their hands full elsewhere, has hurried down the gorge, all the fighting men of the miners' party along with him.

It is but a moment to place the escaped captives behind the rocks standing thick all around; then, screening themselves by the same, they await the coming of the savages. But these come not; enough have they to do looking out for their own safety. The howitzers, now near, are belching forth their bombs, that burst here and there, dealing death in their ranks.

With the red-skins it is no longer a question

of resistance or fight, but flight, *sauve qui peut.*
And without thought of taking along with them
either spoils or captives, they deem it enough if
they can but save their own lives.

They are all on horseback now, their chief
at their head, who in loud command calls upon
them to follow him—not to the charge, but in
retreat.

First they flee northward ; but short is their
ride in that direction. Scarce have they commenced it, when they see in front of them a
body of horse, seemingly numerous as that
they are retreating from.

Shall they meet it, or turn back ? The
thunder guns are still more than a mile from
the abandoned camp, and they will have time
to repass it.

Promptly deciding to do so, they wheel round
and gallop back, *ventra à terre;* not slowing
pace nor drawing rein till they have reached the
western elbow of the lake. Then only coming
to a stop perforce at sight of still another party
of pale-faces there to confront them.

Intercepted, threatened on every side by a far superior force, they now know themselves in a trap. Panicstricken, they would surrender and cry for quarter, but well are they aware it would not be given. So, as wolves brought to bay, they at length determine on fighting—to the death.

For many of them, death it is. Beset on all sides, in the midst of a circle of fire, bombs exploding and bullets raining through their ranks, they make but a despairing resistance; which ends in half their number being killed and the other half taken prisoner.

*　　*　　*　　*　　*

The rescuers are now in possession of the camp, animals, everything. But the first to reach the bottom of the ravine is he who has guided them thither, Henry Tresillian; there to receive a shower of thanks and blessings. his father pressing him to his bosom, which alike beats with joy and pride. And the *gambusino* embraces him, too, crying out,

"I see you've brought back my saddle, señorito; and after the service it has done, I hope you'll never consent to part with it. Bridle and saddle both, I make you a present of them; which I trust you'll do me the honour to accept."

This draws the attention of all upon Crusader standing by, who in turn becomes the recipient of an ovation.

But his young master stays not to witness it. Up on the summit is one who occupies all his thoughts, claiming him now; and up bounds he with lighter heart than he ever before made that ascent.

"Henrique!" "Gertrudes!" are the exchanged exclamations of the youthful lovers, as they become locked in each other's arms, their lips meeting in a kiss of rapturous joy.

*　　*　　*　　*　　*

All congratulations over, the corraled wagons are once more in possession of their owners. Scarce any damage has been done to the mining machinery or tools; the Indians, from neglect or ignorance of their uses, not having thought it worth while to destroy them. And for the animals and chattels they had carried off, there is ample compensation in those now taken from them—enough to furnish the wagons with fresh teams, re-establish the pack-train, in short, put the caravan in order for resuming the march. Which it does, after a couple of days spent in getting things into condition for the route, when it continues on to its original destination, the *gambusino* still with it as guide.

On the same day Requeñes starts out on return to Arispe, taking the Coyotero prisoners along with him; while Don Juliano and his valiant *vaqueros* charge themselves with the task of restoring the women of Nacamori to their homes.

When all are gone, and the Lost Mountain again left to tranquillity and solitude, it is for days the scene of a spectacle telling of the terrible strife which had occurred. The wolves and coyotes have gathered from afar, and over the bodies of the slain savages left unburied, with those of their horses killed in the encounter, hold riot and revel.

There, too, are the black vultures, some in the air, some on the ground, in flocks so thick as to darken both earth and sky. They anticipated a plenteous repast—they have not been disappointed.

CHAPTER XXXIV.

THE last scene of our tale lies in the *pueblita* of Santa Gertrudes; a mining village chiefly supported by the *minera* bearing the same name, whose works, with the specialities of crushing-sheds, smelting-houses, and tall chimneys, are seen just outside its suburbs.

All have a modern look, as well they may. On the ground where they stand, but three years before grew a thick *chapparal* of mezquite, cactus, yucca, and other plants characteristic of desert vegetation. For Santa Gertrudes is in the very heart of the Sonora desert, remote from any other civilized settlement.

Its prosperity, however, has attracted settlers; for not only does the population of the village

299

itself receive constant increase, but many fertile tracts in the country around have been taken up, and are occupied by a goodly number of graziers and agriculturists, whose chief purpose is to supply the comestibles required by the miners and their dependants.

The growth of Santa Gertrudes has been remarkably rapid, almost unprecedently so. From the first opening of the mine, every vein worked has proved a *bonanza*, enriching the owners, Don Estevan Villanueva and Robert Tresillian. For it is the *veta* discovered, denounced, and made over to them by Pedro Vicente.

The gold-seeker himself has also become rich, by the conditions already mentioned as attached to the conveyance of the property. In short, all concerned have benefited thereby— every one of that travelling party delayed, with lives endangered, on the summit of the Cerro Perdido.

In and around Santa Gertrudes—name bestowed in honour of the Señora Villanueva and

her daughter, or rather their patroness saint
—is every evidence of advancement. The
cottages of the miners are trim and clean, the
shops that supply them showing an abundance
of goods, even to articles of *luxe* and adornment. A pretty *capella*, with spire and belfry,
stands central by the side of the public square,
for, as in all Spanish-American towns, Santa
Gertrudes has its *plaza*.

Two other sides of the same are occupied by
houses of superior pretension, with ornamental
grounds — the respective residences of Don
Estevan and his English partner—while here
and there a house larger and better than the
common denotes the dwelling of an official of
the *minera*, some head of a department

On this day Santa Gertrudes is *en fête*. Its
plaza is full of people ; the miners in their gala
dresses, and, mingling with them, *rancheros*—
the new settlers from the country around—
resplendent in their picturesque costume. Soldiers, too, mix with the crowd, in the gay
uniform of the Zacatecas Lancers. For Colonel

Requeñes and his regiment, on return from an expedition to the northern frontier, have halted at the *pueblita*, and are encamped on the plain outside. The tall chimneys of the *minera* send forth no smoke, no sound proceeds from the crushing-sheds or the smelting-houses; all is silent, and work suspended as if it were a Sunday.

Different with the *capilla*, from whose belfry comes a continual clanging of bells—merry bells —marriage bells. Nor needs any one telling who are to be wedded. All know that the owners are about to enter into relations different from that of a mere commercial partnership; that Gertrudes Villanueva is about to become the wife of Henry Tresillian.

The hour for the happy union has at length arrived, and from the two grand houses on the *plaza* issue the bride and bridegroom—each with their train of attendants—and take their way to the *capella*, amidst the enthusiastic plaudits of the assembled people, who cry out,

" *Viva la novia linda ! Viva el novio valiente*

—*nuestro salvador!*" (Long live the beautiful bride! Long live the gallant bridegroom—our saviour!)

Inside the church the ceremony proceeds, relatives and friends from afar assisting at it; among them Don Juliano Romero, and of course, also, Colonel Requeñes. And there is one present who not only disapproves of the marriage, but would forbid it, were it only in his power. This the young cornet of lancers, Colonel Requeñes' aide-de-camp, now a captain, who stands among the spectators, with an expression upon his features telling of a heart torn with jealousy.

How different is that on the face of Pedro Vicente, luminous with delight! Joyed and proud is he to see his young *protégé* of the chase attain the desire of his heart, in its fullest happiness.

The procession returns to the house of the bride's father, followed by the crowd, again vociferating, " *Viva la novia linda! Viva el novio valiente!* "

Then the pre-arranged sports of the day commence on a grassy plain outside the *pueblita*. There is *correr el gallo* (running the cock), *colcar el toro* (baiting the bull), with other feats of equitation, in which Crusader bears a conspicuous part. Ridden by a famous *domidor*— his owner for once but a looker-on—the beautiful black wins every prize, in speed outstripping all horses on the ground.

The Lancer band makes music in accompaniment; and over an improvised pavilion, ornamented with evergreens, in which stand the chief spectators, waves the national flag— that same bit of bunting which, three years before, was run up as a signal of distress on the LOST MOUNTAIN.

THE END.

DALZIEL BROTHERS, CAMDEN PRESS, LONDON, N.W.

www.ingramcontent.com/pod-product-compliance
Lightning Source LLC
Chambersburg PA
CBHW060519030726
47498CB00004B/996